FOR YOU

(A Morgan Cross FBI Suspense Thriller—Book One)

BLAKE PIERCE

Blake Pierce

Blake Pierce is the USA Today bestselling author of the RILEY PAGE mystery series, which includes seventeen books. Blake Pierce is also the author of the MACKENZIE WHITE mystery series, comprising fourteen books; of the AVERY BLACK mystery series, comprising six books; of the KERI LOCKE mystery series, comprising five books; of the MAKING OF RILEY PAIGE mystery series, comprising six books; of the KATE WISE mystery series, comprising seven books; of the CHLOE FINE psychological suspense mystery, comprising six books; of the JESSIE HUNT psychological suspense thriller series, comprising twenty-eight books; of the AU PAIR psychological suspense thriller series, comprising three books; of the ZOE PRIME mystery series, comprising six books; of the ADELE SHARP mystery series, comprising sixteen books, of the EUROPEAN VOYAGE cozy mystery series, comprising six books; of the LAURA FROST FBI suspense thriller, comprising eleven books; of the ELLA DARK FBI suspense thriller, comprising fourteen books (and counting); of the A YEAR IN EUROPE cozy mystery series, comprising nine books, of the AVA GOLD mystery series, comprising six books; of the RACHEL GIFT mystery series, comprising ten books (and counting); of the VALERIE LAW mystery series, comprising nine books (and counting); of the PAIGE KING mystery series, comprising eight books (and counting); of the MAY MOORE mystery series, comprising eleven books; of the CORA SHIELDS mystery series, comprising eight books (and counting); of the NICKY LYONS mystery series, comprising eight books (and counting), of the CAMI LARK mystery series, comprising eight books (and counting), of the AMBER YOUNG mystery series, comprising five books (and counting), of the DAISY FORTUNE mystery series, comprising five books (and counting), of the FIONA RED mystery series, comprising five books (and counting), of the FAITH BOLD mystery series, comprising five books (and counting), of the JULIETTE HART mystery series, comprising five books (and counting), of the MORGAN CROSS mystery series, comprising five books (and counting), and of the new FINN WRIGHT mystery series, comprising five books (and counting).

An avid reader and lifelong fan of the mystery and thriller genres, Blake loves to hear from you, so please feel free to visit www.blakepierceauthor.com to learn more and stay in touch.

ISBN: 978-1-0943-7907-4

BOOKS BY BLAKE PIERCE

FINN WRIGHT MYSTERY SERIES
WHEN YOU'RE MINE (Book #1)
WHEN YOU'RE SAFE (Book #2)
WHEN YOU'RE CLOSE (Book #3)
WHEN YOU'RE SLEEPING (Book #4)
WHEN YOU'RE SANE (Book #5)

MORGAN CROSS MYSTERY SERIES
FOR YOU (Book #1)
FOR RAGE (Book #2)
FOR LUST (Book #3)
FOR WRATH (Book #4)
FOREVER (Book #5)

JULIETTE HART MYSTERY SERIES
NOTHING TO FEAR (Book #1)
NOTHING THERE (Book #2)
NOTHING WATCHING (Book #3)
NOTHING HIDING (Book #4)
NOTHING LEFT (Book #5)

FAITH BOLD MYSTERY SERIES
SO LONG (Book #1)
SO COLD (Book #2)
SO SCARED (Book #3)
SO NORMAL (Book #4)
SO FAR GONE (Book #5)

FIONA RED MYSTERY SERIES
LET HER GO (Book #1)
LET HER BE (Book #2)
LET HER HOPE (Book #3)

LET HER WISH (Book #4)
LET HER LIVE (Book #5)

DAISY FORTUNE MYSTERY SERIES
NEED YOU (Book #1)
CLAIM YOU (Book #2)
CRAVE YOU (Book #3)
CHOOSE YOU (Book #4)
CHASE YOU (Book #5)

AMBER YOUNG MYSTERY SERIES
ABSENT PITY (Book #1)
ABSENT REMORSE (Book #2)
ABSENT FEELING (Book #3)
ABSENT MERCY (Book #4)
ABSENT REASON (Book #5)

CAMI LARK MYSTERY SERIES
JUST ME (Book #1)
JUST OUTSIDE (Book #2)
JUST RIGHT (Book #3)
JUST FORGET (Book #4)
JUST ONCE (Book #5)
JUST HIDE (Book #6)
JUST NOW (Book #7)
JUST HOPE (Book #8)

NICKY LYONS MYSTERY SERIES
ALL MINE (Book #1)
ALL HIS (Book #2)
ALL HE SEES (Book #3)
ALL ALONE (Book #4)
ALL FOR ONE (Book #5)
ALL HE TAKES (Book #6)
ALL FOR ME (Book #7)
ALL IN (Book #8)

CORA SHIELDS MYSTERY SERIES
UNDONE (Book #1)
UNWANTED (Book #2)

UNHINGED (Book #3)
UNSAID (Book #4)
UNGLUED (Book #5)
UNSTABLE (Book #6)
UNKNOWN (Book #7)
UNAWARE (Book #8)

MAY MOORE SUSPENSE THRILLER
NEVER RUN (Book #1)
NEVER TELL (Book #2)
NEVER LIVE (Book #3)
NEVER HIDE (Book #4)
NEVER FORGIVE (Book #5)
NEVER AGAIN (Book #6)
NEVER LOOK BACK (Book #7)
NEVER FORGET (Book #8)
NEVER LET GO (Book #9)
NEVER PRETEND (Book #10)
NEVER HESITATE (Book #11)

PAIGE KING MYSTERY SERIES
THE GIRL HE PINED (Book #1)
THE GIRL HE CHOSE (Book #2)
THE GIRL HE TOOK (Book #3)
THE GIRL HE WISHED (Book #4)
THE GIRL HE CROWNED (Book #5)
THE GIRL HE WATCHED (Book #6)
THE GIRL HE WANTED (Book #7)
THE GIRL HE CLAIMED (Book #8)

VALERIE LAW MYSTERY SERIES
NO MERCY (Book #1)
NO PITY (Book #2)
NO FEAR (Book #3)
NO SLEEP (Book #4)
NO QUARTER (Book #5)
NO CHANCE (Book #6)
NO REFUGE (Book #7)
NO GRACE (Book #8)
NO ESCAPE (Book #9)

GIRL, MISSING (Book #13)
GIRL, UNKNOWN (Book #14)

LAURA FROST FBI SUSPENSE THRILLER
ALREADY GONE (Book #1)
ALREADY SEEN (Book #2)
ALREADY TRAPPED (Book #3)
ALREADY MISSING (Book #4)
ALREADY DEAD (Book #5)
ALREADY TAKEN (Book #6)
ALREADY CHOSEN (Book #7)
ALREADY LOST (Book #8)
ALREADY HIS (Book #9)
ALREADY LURED (Book #10)
ALREADY COLD (Book #11)

EUROPEAN VOYAGE COZY MYSTERY SERIES
MURDER (AND BAKLAVA) (Book #1)
DEATH (AND APPLE STRUDEL) (Book #2)
CRIME (AND LAGER) (Book #3)
MISFORTUNE (AND GOUDA) (Book #4)
CALAMITY (AND A DANISH) (Book #5)
MAYHEM (AND HERRING) (Book #6)

ADELE SHARP MYSTERY SERIES
LEFT TO DIE (Book #1)
LEFT TO RUN (Book #2)
LEFT TO HIDE (Book #3)
LEFT TO KILL (Book #4)
LEFT TO MURDER (Book #5)
LEFT TO ENVY (Book #6)
LEFT TO LAPSE (Book #7)
LEFT TO VANISH (Book #8)
LEFT TO HUNT (Book #9)
LEFT TO FEAR (Book #10)
LEFT TO PREY (Book #11)
LEFT TO LURE (Book #12)
LEFT TO CRAVE (Book #13)
LEFT TO LOATHE (Book #14)
LEFT TO HARM (Book #15)

LEFT TO RUIN (Book #16)

THE AU PAIR SERIES
ALMOST GONE (Book#1)
ALMOST LOST (Book #2)
ALMOST DEAD (Book #3)

ZOE PRIME MYSTERY SERIES
FACE OF DEATH (Book#1)
FACE OF MURDER (Book #2)
FACE OF FEAR (Book #3)
FACE OF MADNESS (Book #4)
FACE OF FURY (Book #5)
FACE OF DARKNESS (Book #6)

A JESSIE HUNT PSYCHOLOGICAL SUSPENSE SERIES
THE PERFECT WIFE (Book #1)
THE PERFECT BLOCK (Book #2)
THE PERFECT HOUSE (Book #3)
THE PERFECT SMILE (Book #4)
THE PERFECT LIE (Book #5)
THE PERFECT LOOK (Book #6)
THE PERFECT AFFAIR (Book #7)
THE PERFECT ALIBI (Book #8)
THE PERFECT NEIGHBOR (Book #9)
THE PERFECT DISGUISE (Book #10)
THE PERFECT SECRET (Book #11)
THE PERFECT FAÇADE (Book #12)
THE PERFECT IMPRESSION (Book #13)
THE PERFECT DECEIT (Book #14)
THE PERFECT MISTRESS (Book #15)
THE PERFECT IMAGE (Book #16)
THE PERFECT VEIL (Book #17)
THE PERFECT INDISCRETION (Book #18)
THE PERFECT RUMOR (Book #19)
THE PERFECT COUPLE (Book #20)
THE PERFECT MURDER (Book #21)
THE PERFECT HUSBAND (Book #22)
THE PERFECT SCANDAL (Book #23)
THE PERFECT MASK (Book #24)

ONCE LOST (Book #10)
ONCE BURIED (Book #11)
ONCE BOUND (Book #12)
ONCE TRAPPED (Book #13)
ONCE DORMANT (Book #14)
ONCE SHUNNED (Book #15)
ONCE MISSED (Book #16)
ONCE CHOSEN (Book #17)

MACKENZIE WHITE MYSTERY SERIES
BEFORE HE KILLS (Book #1)
BEFORE HE SEES (Book #2)
BEFORE HE COVETS (Book #3)
BEFORE HE TAKES (Book #4)
BEFORE HE NEEDS (Book #5)
BEFORE HE FEELS (Book #6)
BEFORE HE SINS (Book #7)
BEFORE HE HUNTS (Book #8)
BEFORE HE PREYS (Book #9)
BEFORE HE LONGS (Book #10)
BEFORE HE LAPSES (Book #11)
BEFORE HE ENVIES (Book #12)
BEFORE HE STALKS (Book #13)
BEFORE HE HARMS (Book #14)

AVERY BLACK MYSTERY SERIES
CAUSE TO KILL (Book #1)
CAUSE TO RUN (Book #2)
CAUSE TO HIDE (Book #3)
CAUSE TO FEAR (Book #4)
CAUSE TO SAVE (Book #5)
CAUSE TO DREAD (Book #6)

KERI LOCKE MYSTERY SERIES
A TRACE OF DEATH (Book #1)
A TRACE OF MURDER (Book #2)
A TRACE OF VICE (Book #3)
A TRACE OF CRIME (Book #4)
A TRACE OF HOPE (Book #5)

CHAPTER ONE

Morgan walked slowly down the prison corridor, relishing the sound of the tin cups slamming against the cell bars. It rose in a cacophony, prisoners all around her cheering and whooping, clearly wishing that they could be the ones to be let free on this day.

Morgan tried hard not to think of the last ten years as she went. She forced herself not to look back, whatever she did, as if looking back might change the warden's mind.

Of course, she knew this was silly. Finally, she had been vindicated, proven not guilty. The entire world knew now that she had never done it, that her career as an FBI agent with the Behavioral Analysis Unit had been stolen from her, that ten precious years of her life had been essentially erased.

She did wonder, though, what had taken so long. She knew there were a few people at the bureau who had consistently worked toward proving her innocence. She still wasn't one hundred percent certain what had been the smoking gun—something to do with mishandled files and speculation of conspiracy. She could get to all of that later, though.

For right now, she had a life to get back on track.

She walked, and walked, and wondered: what now? Images of the last ten hard years in prison flashed through her mind.

The memories were painful, but Morgan couldn't help but feel grateful for the people who had stood by her through it all. She thought of her father, there every week, no matter what. She fought back a tear as she thought of his death, the one person she had been looking forward to seeing most, robbed from her two years before her release.

Her old partner from the BAU had come by every now and then, too. More than she'd expected, to be honest. He'd been one of the driving forces behind making sure she didn't stay in prison for the entirety of her twenty-five-year sentence. But despite all of that, she knew she'd missed so much—that a huge portion of her life had been taken from her.

The thoughts of her years in prison gave way to a feeling of anger. She had been robbed of the best years of her life, and she had a score to settle. She couldn't wait to get out of those doors and start a new life.

1

She had a list of people she needed to see, people who had put her there, people who had lied to the jury and to the judge.

Morgan's heart was pounding with a new sense of purpose. She walked faster, eager to get out and start her quest for revenge. She had a plan, a plan to make them pay. She had learned a lot in prison, and she knew how to use the things she'd learned. She'd gathered a whole new skillset and a better understanding of how criminals operated and thought. If she could fall back into her old job (if they'd have her) she thought it would go a very long way to help further develop her approach.

The cheers of the prisoners faded in the distance as she approached the end of the corridor. She could see the light shining through the door, and she knew that her new life was waiting for her on the other side. She took a deep breath, opened the door, and stepped outside.

The Texas sun was shining bright, and the smell of freedom was in the air. She could not hear the traffic and thriving heartbeat of the Dallas–Fort Worth area from where she stood just outside of the prison, but she knew it was there. She'd always felt it, a shadow against the prison, a reminder of her former life.

Morgan closed her eyes and took a deep breath. She felt alive again, and she knew that she had a purpose. She turned around and looked back at the prison. She would never forget those years, but they were now a part of her past. As she'd prepared for her release, she didn't think this moment would impact her so much, but she suddenly found herself on the verge of tears.

A bus pulled up unceremoniously, a prisoner transport, and stopped in front of her, its brakes squealing.

It would take her home, she knew. Well, it was really her father's home, but during the wretched process of dealing with his death, she had been informed that he had left her his house and all of the money in his checking and savings accounts. It almost seemed fitting that the only thing left of her prior existence was the house she'd grown up in.

It was her only place left in the world.

And going back there was the one thing she dreaded the most.

***

Morgan stood before her old house, a simple ranch on a generic suburban street, and stared. It was smaller than she remembered, darker, less well-kept. She could see the layers of dirt on the peeling paint, the knee-high weeds covering the lawn. The neighbors must have

2

hated that, she mused. The property taxes were overdue, she knew, and she'd need to sort that out as soon as possible.

Morgan knew she should feel a sense of comfort seeing the house, but she did not. It brought back memories of her old life, snatched away from her. The life she should have had.

She slowly approached the door. She reached under the flowerpot and took out the key from the place she knew her dad would have left it.

She smiled. Still there. Rusted. But there.

She took a deep breath and opened the door.

She braced herself and went inside.

The smell hit her first, a musty odor that seemed to emanate from every surface. The house was dimly lit, the curtains drawn, and Morgan had to squint to see in the shadows. There was a layer of dust on everything, and cobwebs hung from the ceiling. The furniture was old and worn, and she could see where mice had chewed through the corners of the sofa. It had only been abandoned for two years—since her father had passed away—but it looked as if it had been neglected for much longer.

Maybe for as long as my prison sentence, she thought.

She hated that she'd still been in prison when her father had died. She'd been allowed to view the funeral from a distance but that was all. And even then, she'd felt guilty even though she hadn't killed anyone...even though she was completely innocent. She'd felt guilty for not being there with her father in his final days. She hated that his final breath on this Earth was spent knowing that his daughter was in prison.

He'd never believed she'd done it, of course. He'd firmly known that she'd been framed—very likely by the same man she'd been chasing down at the time of her arrest. He'd attested to this in his visits and letters.

She had to shake the thought of him away as she walked through the house. It was going to feel far too much like being haunted if she allowed the memory of him to follow her inside.

It was like being in a time capsule, a memory of a life that no longer existed.

The house was just like she remembered it, and yet completely different.

She walked down the hall, past the picture on the wall of her and her father on one of their fishing trips, and into the kitchen. The cabinets were empty, the refrigerator was unplugged, and there was mold growing on the countertop.

Morgan felt a wave of sadness wash over her. This had been her home, and she had lost it all. She had lost her father, her career, her life. She had nothing left but this house, and even that was falling apart.

Morgan's heart sank as she walked through the living room, past the old television set, the worn-out couch, and the bookshelves filled with her father's old books. She couldn't bear to look at them, not now. Not after what had happened.

But then she saw something that made her heart skip a beat. On the coffee table. An envelope, addressed to her.

She picked it up and tore it open.

"Dear Morgan," it read. *"If you're reading this, it means you've been released. I always knew you were innocent, and I'm sorry that I didn't live long enough to see you come home. But I wanted to leave you something. All my love. Forever, Dad."*

"Forever," she said out loud.

He'd known he was going to die and had still used terms like *forever*. It had been prostate cancer. It had come on quickly and they'd caught it late. After chemo had nearly destroyed his will to live for a few weeks, he opted not to go that route.

Two and a half months later, he was dead. And all she'd taken away from it was a distant view from the other side of a church parking lot as blurry shapes milled around his gravesite.

She looked back inside the envelope and her heart fell to see an old Polaroid of them together. Sailing. And behind the photo, cash. A thousand dollars. It pained her to think of how hard he'd have had to work for that.

Her heart broke, and a sob escaped her.

It was too much. The memories. The darkness. The lost years. She felt suffocated by it all.

Morgan collapsed onto the couch and cried, tears streaming down her face. She had lost so much, but her father's love and support had never wavered. Even in death, he had found a way to comfort her, to let her know that she was loved.

She wiped her tears away and took a deep breath, feeling a sense of calm wash over her. Resolve.

There was only one thing she knew she could do.

And only one thing she knew that was left in this house that could still be put to use.

She made her way down the short dark hall to the bathroom.

The medicine cabinet.

She opened it and stared. Sure enough, the pill bottles were still there. She was certain the pills inside were long expired, but did that really matter? She didn't think so. With trembling hands and tears still in her eyes, she reached inside and grabbed one of the old bottles.

She popped the top and peered inside. The white pills seemed to greet her warmly. She rattled them a bit, as if trying to communicate. There were at least a dozen. She wasn't sure if that would be enough.

But there was one easy way to find out.

She let out a gasp and tilted the bottle to her mouth.

She nearly yelled out when a loud banging noise tore through the house. For a very strange moment, she was sure it was her father, or at least the ghost of her father, not approving of what she was about to do.

But then, shaking and still crying a bit, she realized what she'd heard. And in a way, it was just as alarming as the idea of her father's ghost watching what she was about to do.

It was a knock at the front door.

CHAPTER TWO

Morgan put the cap back on the pills, doing her best to keep the feeling of guilt from taking over. What the hell had she been thinking?

She put the bottle back inside the medicine cabinet and closed it, giving it one last, longing look. She then made her way through the house as the knock at the door came again. This time, a voice accompanied it. It was the voice of an older woman, slightly rough as it came through the closed front door.

"Hello?"

Morgan knew the voice and it brought a brief spark of joy to her heart. The voice was hoarse from years of chain smoking. It was the voice of Lora Foster, her next-door neighbor. She'd thought of Lora often while in prison, but ever since the news of her release, she hadn't given the old woman much thought. She had to be at least eighty now.

And if it was Lora, that meant Morgan was going to be met with either good news or bad news on the other side of the door. Lora had been the one to keep her pit bull when she'd gone to prison. Skunk had been barely more than a puppy when Morgan had been arrested. Ten years was a long time, but she figured there was a good chance Skunk was still alive.

Anxious to see both Lora and Skunk, Morgan opened the door.

And there she was, Lora Foster with a much older Skunk in tow. The old woman's face was lined with worry and age, but her eyes sparkled when she saw Morgan. Lora was leaning on a cane and Skunk was wagging his tail so hard his entire body shook. Morgan wasn't sure if the dog remembered her or not. Maybe he was just so excited because Lora was.

"Morgan!" Lora exclaimed, her voice filled with joy. "It's so good to see you!"

"Lora..."

The two women hugged immediately. But Lora seemed more interested in taking a good, long look at the neighbor she hadn't seen in nearly a decade. She broke the hug quickly and looked Morgan over in amazement and shock.

"You look so different," she said, her voice barely a whisper.

6

Morgan knew that was true. She had lost weight in prison, and her hair had grown longer. She was wearing clothes that were too big for her, and she knew that she looked a little worse for wear.

"I'm sure I do. But…I'm good."

Skunk was sniffing at the doorway and stepped inside a few paces. Morgan knelt down and hugged the old dog, tears streaming down her face. He seemed happy enough to get the attention but so far, there didn't seem to be any recognition.

"I've missed you, boy," she whispered.

Lora came closer and took Morgan's hand. "I heard you were coming back," she said. "I wanted to be here to welcome you home."

Morgan's heart swelled with gratitude. Lora had been one of the few people who had believed in her innocence through the entire ordeal.

"Lora, I can't thank you enough for taking care of him while I was away."

"Are you kidding? Skunk and I…we kept each other sane."

Morgan then remembered that Lora's husband had died just two months before she'd been arrested and sent to prison. When Morgan had asked Lora to take care of Skunk, she'd been honored. It was, Morgan had always assumed, a way to help Lora get over her loss. And she'd assumed Skunk would have led a good, comfortable life with Lora…that he'd probably have lived up his life—or most of it—by the time she was released from prison.

"How are you holding up?" Lora said.

"I don't know yet," Morgan answered, thinking about the pills in the bathroom and what she'd almost done less than three minutes ago.

"I suppose not. I mean, I can't even imagine what you must be going through. And…well, of course, I was just wrecked to hear about your father. I'm so sorry, Morgan."

"Thanks," she said. She was about two deep breaths away from crying—from crumbling into pieces and sobbing on the floor.

"Of course, you know I'm here for you. Whatever you need."

"I know. Thank you so much. I know you were here, helping Dad try to keep this place looking somewhat presentable."

"I was. But when he passed away and it came down to me…well, you saw the state of the grass outside. And…well," she said, waving a hand around dismissively. "I cleaned it once or twice after he passed but after a while…I know it's selfish, but I just couldn't bring myself to do it."

"Oh, you did more than enough," Morgan said. "I truly…"

But she wasn't sure what to say. She had Skunk back and even if he didn't recognize her, he seemed to like her. She had her home back. Those things…they were something, at least.

"I read up on how to handle you," Lora said, looking guilty.

"What do you mean?"

"Someone coming home from prison after a decade…should I smother you with attention and kindness or let you adjust slowly and let you ask for those things when you need them."

Oh," Morgan said, smiling thinly. "And what did you find?"

"That I need to let you come to me. Too much attention and affection right away can be a bad thing. I'm supposed to let you get accustomed to familiar things from your old life. Like the house, for instance." She chuckled and then, petting Skunk, said: "Or a pet."

Morgan nodded, giving Skunk more scratches. He looked back and forth between the women, loving every second of the attention. "At the risk of sounding rude, that's a pretty accurate answer," Morgan said.

"I figured. And no offense taken. You know where I am. So if you need me, you wade yourself through that jungle of a yard and come get me."

With that, Lora placed a delicate kiss on Morgan's cheek and started for the door. Skunk obediently went after her, but Lora halted the dog in its tracks.

"No, sir," she said. "You stay here. Get reacquainted with your real master."

Skunk's tail wagged, but uncertainly.

"I appreciate it," Morgan said. "But this is all new to him, too. Would you mind if we did a sort of warm-up process? He's seen me, got a few sniffs in. Maybe bring him over again tomorrow and the day after that, and the day after that, and so on. Once he gets really used to me, we can try a transition. Or…you can keep him. You said he kept you sane."

"He did. But now it's time for him to keep you sane. And your warm-up idea sounds perfectly fine to me. But let's let him hang out here for a bit without me. Is that okay?"

"Of course."

Lora smiled and finally made her exit. Skunk whined a bit when Lora left, taking a few uncertain steps toward the door. He then turned to Morgan and gave her an inquisitive look.

"Do you remember me, boy?"

The dog walked over and sniffed at her, his tail still wagging. And for now, she supposed that would be good enough.

8

"I don't have any chow," she said. "For either of us, now that I think about it."

And as that thought sank in, she realized that now, on her first day back, she was already going to have to start tackling everyday chores. Little things like grocery trips and cleaning the house. She'd eventually have to get out and mow the lawn.

As she tried to wrap her mind around all of this, there was another knock on the door. She frowned, but in a good-natured way. She hadn't expected Lora to be able to stay away. Her kind heart would insist on doing everything she could, flirting with being intrusive just to make sure Morgan was doing well.

She answered the door with Skunk trotting along by her side. She opened the door, fully prepared to make a smart-ass but kind remark about Lora's kindness. But Lora wasn't on the other side of the door.

It was another familiar face...one she'd thought she might never see again.

Derik Greene, her partner of three years with the BAU. For a second, she could have sworn she was dreaming. It was a shock to her system, this part of her old life so suddenly showing up at her door.

"Hey," was all he said.

Morgan suddenly felt swimmy-headed as she looked at him.

She hadn't expected to see Derik again, especially not on her first day back. She had thought about him often during her time in prison, wondering if he still thought about her, if he still believed she was innocent. He had, after all, testified on her behalf in court. She assumed that had caused tons of problems for him at work. When she'd gone to prison, her entire department had been divided—about half thought she was guilty, that she had assisted a serial killer with his gruesome work. The other half, primarily led by Derik, had done their best to prove her innocence.

She'd assumed that since then, Derik would have moved on to bigger and better things. He was an exceptional agent and she figured he'd have a cozy director's job at their field office by the time she got out.

"Derik," she said, her voice barely above a whisper.

He looked the same as he had before, his dark hair neatly combed to the side, his piercing blue eyes locked on hers. He was dressed for work, the black jacket over the white button-down. The neat, straight-legged pants that weren't quite slacks.

But there was something different about him now, something that she couldn't quite put her finger on.

9

"I wasn't sure if it would be okay to come this early," he said.

"How did you even know I was out?"

He looked at her, slightly befuddled. "Morgan...I've been keeping track. I've had this day on my calendar for a while now. If I didn't think it would have embarrassed you, I would have been at the prison to pick you up."

"Oh." She had no idea what else to say, so she simply stood aside and gestured for him to come in.

Derik took a step forward, and Skunk barked excitedly, wagging his tail even harder. Morgan reached down and scratched the dog behind the ears, trying to calm him down. Morgan wanted to ask Derik so many questions, to find out what he had been up to for the past ten years, but she couldn't bring herself to do it.

"How have you been?" she asked Derik, trying to break the awkward silence that had settled between them.

"Good. Busy."

"Any cases worth talking about?"

He grinned at her as they settled on her couch. It smelled musty from years of non-use. "You really want to talk about work?"

"Well, it's not my work anymore."

He shrugged and looked around the house, then his eyes settled on her. "Are you doing okay, Morgan?"

"Yeah, why?"

"Honestly? You look...I don't know. What's the word for someone who looks like they're depressed as hell but also jacked. Jesus, did you work out every day?"

"Not every day, but most days."

She noticed the strange tension between them instantly. It had never been there before; it was a wedge created by the last ten years. Surely he felt it, too. It made her wonder why he was here at all. It wasn't like Derik to drop by unannounced. Though, without a new phone number for her and no real organization to her life yet, how else would he have reached out?

"I...I'm sorry it was a while between visits there at the end," he said.

"It's okay, Derik. You had a life. A job, a wife. You came more than enough."

"Thirty-one visits in ten years," he said. "I kept count just in case I needed to hold it against you. Also...as of right now, there's only the job. The wife...that ended a long time ago."

"And you didn't tell me?"

"When, during one of my visits? It's not exactly uplifting talk to share with a friend and work partner who's been wrongly accused and thrown into jail."

"What happened?"

"We got bored. Just sort of drifted apart."

"Just like that?" Morgan asked skeptically. She had a feeling Derik wasn't telling her the whole truth.

He waved the comment away. "I'd really rather not talk about it."

She was relieved to see the glimpse of his old self, of the humor he was always so quick to toss out if a situation got too uncomfortable. Even though there was nothing funny about his avoidance of the topic, his tone was practically dripping with it. But it felt forced, not natural at all. Something was off. And in that moment, as she noticed that he was finding it hard to look directly at her, Morgan started to get a very bad feeling.

"What is it, Derik? Why are you really here? And ten years or not, I know you too well. Your poker face sucks, you know."

He sighed and finally looked at her again, their eyes locking. She saw sadness in his gaze and something that looked like...what? Was that excitement, maybe? Without taking his eyes from her, he reached into the inside of his jacket and pulled out an envelope. It had been folded to a curve, standard paper-size.

"There's a case," he said. "And I was sent to tell you about it. To ask you if you've thought about coming back."

Red-hot fury passed through her. If she hadn't missed Derik so much over the last ten years, she would have punched him in the face.

"I hope to God you're kidding," she said, trying to control the waver in her voice.

"I wish I was, but no. There's a whole panel...three directors and a supervisor. When this whole thing started," he said, shaking the envelope, "they all realized you'd be out soon and that you'd be—"

"No."

He nodded and took a deep breath. "I figured that would be your reaction. And I told them as much. But all the same, you really should at least read about it. Or let me tell you what—"

"Get out, Derik," she said, getting to her feet.

She was angrier than she'd been in a very long time but God, she didn't really want him to go. Unlike Lora, she knew Derik was great for just sitting and simply being there.

"Morgan..."

"Out!"

When he got to his feet, envelope still in hand, she walked directly behind him. She ushered him through the door and when he turned to say something else, she slammed it in his face.

Even with the door closed, she could tell he was still standing there. She knew she'd possibly overreacted but she was fine with that for right now.

She was fine with it until he spoke from the other side of the door.

"Morgan…he's back. Samson…"

Surely, Morgan thought, this was a dream. It had to be. Maybe she was still back in prison, having one hell of a nightmare just before she was to be released.

Samson…back. There was no way. The man she'd been after ten years ago. The lunatic that had gotten away. And the man she'd been accused of helping. The fact that he'd gone cold and into hiding during her imprisonment hadn't helped her case much.

But the name chilled her. It actually sent about a million different emotions rushing through her. Samson was, after all, the reason she'd been sent to jail.

"Samson is back, Morgan, and we need you."

"Get…the fuck…out of here!" she screamed. She punched the door hard enough for a scattering of dust to fall from the frame and to draw blood from her knuckles.

Skunk barked in protest, making anxious circles on the floor where he'd been potty-trained as a pup.

Morgan felt a wave of tears and grief coming and knew she wouldn't be able to stop them. As she slowly sank to the floor, she heard a soft thump from the other side of the door. She knew it was the sound of Derik leaving the envelope for her.

She wept, managing to keep it quiet. She didn't want Derik to hear it. She concentrated as well as she could and didn't let it out uninterrupted until she heard the sound of a car door closing from the driveway and then the sound of an engine carrying the car away.

She started wailing then, and Skunk came over for support. But even then, as she cried harder than she could remember crying in her life, Morgan was unable to resist.

Her face streaked with tears and a wave of anger flowing through her like lava, she opened the door and took the envelope.

CHAPTER THREE

The Seven Signs Killer. It wasn't a name she'd ever liked, but it was what the media had given to the man who called himself Samson. No last name, just Samson. But that hadn't been juicy enough. The media had far preferred the Seven Signs Killer. It was catchier and sold papers and caused clicks.

When she finally got control of herself, Morgan took the envelope to the kitchen. She sat at the table, not sure if she would be able to handle it. She knew there was no reason Derik would lie about such a thing, so it had to be real.

But her life had ended with the Seven Signs Killer, causing her to go to jail and lose ten years of her life. It seemed like a very strange sort of masochism to fling herself right back into his demented world the day she regained her freedom.

She opened the envelope but stopped there. Did she really need to do this? Did she really want this to once again consume her life?

Ah, but it wasn't as simple as that. The Seven Signs Killer was linked to her prison sentence. But Samson had never been caught. She couldn't help but wonder, for the thousandth time, exactly how Samson had framed her so perfectly.

Without taking the contents out of the envelope, Morgan ran it all back through her head, boiling it down. Samson was a deranged serial killer who believed the messiah desperately wanted to come to earth but, in order for him to come, the seven signs of the messiah needed to be heralded. Samson had taken it upon himself to do it, going on a murdering spree that had started with his interpretation of changing water into wine.

That event alone had resulted in the murder of four people in the form of poisoning. Another dozen or so had gone to the hospital.

Morgan shuddered at the thought of Samson's twisted beliefs and actions. The Seven Signs Killer had caused so much devastation, so much pain and suffering. And now he was back. It was almost as if he'd waited to start things up as soon as she'd gotten out of prison.

And maybe, she thought, that was exactly what he'd done.

But for right now, she didn't see how that was her problem. She had to start fitting into the real world again. She had this house to care for, a dead father to properly grieve. There were calls to make in order to unfreeze her bank accounts, to get phone service, to update everything at the DMV related to driving.

First, though, she had to face this house. She had to face the memories and the emptiness. She also needed to wash the sheets and get a better feel for how the place was maintained, but that was the least of her concerns for the moment.

Ignoring the envelope for the time being, she allowed herself a moment to walk through the house—through each room and the hallway. She could still feel her father in most of the areas, but the dust and neglect tainted the feeling.

When she walked into what had been his bedroom—what she supposed was now her bedroom if she so desired—she simply stood in its center for a moment. She felt the need to cry but knew she wouldn't. She'd never been a big crier and as bad as it sounded, she knew she was all out of tears for her father. Those tears had all been spilled in the weeks following his funeral, crying alone in the darkness of her cell and wondering what life might be like for her when she got out.

She slowly walked toward his small closet and opened the door. A few of his clothes were still hanging up, mostly flannel shirts and button-downs. At the top of the closet, there were a few shoeboxes that she knew served as layman safes; they held copies of her father's social security card and birth certificate, paperwork pertaining to the house, insurance papers, and bank statements.

Beside them, there were two board games: Scrabble and chess. She and her father had played them both so much that some of the chess pieces had started to lose their color, and the Scrabble board was scarred and slightly warped.

As if running on pure instinct, she took the Scrabble board down. She opened the box and unfolded the board on the bed. She shook the velvet bag, the clinking of the tiles inside like sweet, nostalgic music. She then poured them out onto the board, just to hear the sound.

She doubted these tiles would ever get touched again, the board never to be used. It was essentially a part of her life that she could consider closed. Even if she did ever date someone or even if, somewhere down the road, she had kids...she'd never be able to play these with them. It would hurt too much. It would...

"No," she said. She honestly wasn't sure why she'd said it. She'd felt a sting of defiance at the thought of her future, at the thought of things being closed off to her because of past pains.

14

And as she frowned, scattering the tiles around the board, she could feel her father's presence there, a bit stronger. She could recall playing with him as a young girl—maybe nine or ten years old—and asking him to define some of the longer, odder words he would sometimes use. She could especially remember the day she'd asked him to define the word "juxtapose" and then actually made him get the dictionary so she could check just to make sure he wasn't cheating.

When she'd apologized for her doubts, he'd simply laughed and given her a hug. "Don't say you're sorry for that," he'd told her. "Whenever you aren't sure of something, you do whatever you need to get the answer...even if you think it might make some people grumpy."

It was some of the best advice she'd ever gotten, though she'd not known it at the time.

She smirked as she started plinking the tiles back into the pouch one by one. Maybe her father was more present in this house than she thought.

Whenever you aren't sure of something, you do whatever you need to get the answer...

She knew what she had to do.

She couldn't let Samson continue his reign of terror, not when she had the opportunity to stop him. She knew she was rusty and out of practice. She knew she was not in the right mindset to take on such a task.

But maybe she could at least be of some help. And besides, she needed those answers. How had he managed to frame her as if she'd been assisting him? And why had he stopped killing when she'd gone to prison only to start again, a decade later, when she was back out?

Maybe some of the answers were in the envelope Derik had left behind.

She took a deep breath as she headed back to the kitchen. She sat down at the table and pulled out the contents of the envelope.

There were photos of the most recent crime scene, articles, and police reports. Morgan looked through them all with a mix of horror and determination. When she'd nearly stopped him before, he'd accomplished four of the so-called signs. The most recent, from just three days ago, was Samson's representation of Jesus Christ walking on water.

The case photos showed three drowned bodies on the banks of the Kisanthum River. A fourth had been stripped totally naked, draped in a thin white cloth, and tied to a tree.

She shuddered and pushed the stack of papers away.

15

It was enough to make the decision for her. There was simply no way she could help. However…if there was an entire panel relying on her, it meant they were out of answers. Maybe they finally realized she'd been right all those years ago. Maybe they were ready to eat some humble pie and admit she had been right, that they'd been too lackadaisical about the case, and would let her bring this bastard in.

But how could she do it? She had just been released from prison, her life was in shambles, and she had no resources or connections. She didn't even have a single meal in the fridge and wasn't sure how she was supposed to be making money or getting back on her feet.

Of course, there was another easy option. It was waiting for her in the bathroom, in that old prescription bottle. She also had her small storage locker on the other side of town with her old Sig Sauer. A well-placed bullet in her mouth would put thoughts of Samson, the Seven Signs Killer, right out of her mind.

A whining noise broke her quickly out of such thoughts. She turned and saw Skunk sitting at the entry between the kitchen and living room. As she turned, she again noticed the stagnant and filthy state of the kitchen.

Her father would be disappointed if she left all of this, if she gave up and left Skunk with Lora again. If she let this house go to ruin. He'd be so disappointed if she gave up.

"What do you say, boy?" she asked. "You want me to stick around?"

He wagged his tail a bit and gave a sloppy smile that only pit bulls are capable of. He whined again indicating that yeah, he wanted her to stick around and it would be great if it started with her letting him outside to pee.

"Fine, then," she said. "But I need to clean this house. And then maybe I'll head back to the office."

Saying it out loud was surreal. But at the same time, there was the tiniest little flutter in her heart. Excitement? Nostalgia? She wasn't sure. But hearing the words out of her mouth felt right.

And when she thought of hunting down the Seven Signs Killer again, that felt right, too.

She looked back at the envelope and papers on the table, thinking it might be just what she needed to get back on her feet. What better way to do that than to tie up a delayed loose end she'd left behind ten years ago?

***

16

Ten years had not removed the familiarity of the FBI field office. The simple brick exterior, the well-maintained shrubs, the simple sidewalk that led from the parking lot to the front door…it felt as if she'd been here just last week. She supposed that didn't say much about her life before prison. She'd spent so much time in this building that it truly had felt like a second home.

She stepped through the entrance and realized that it all felt the same. It felt like being welcomed home, like a much kinder and spiritual version of a visit from Lora. The morning sun shone through the large arc-shaped windows over the front entrance, gleaming off of the faux-marble floor.

God, she'd missed this.

It was a strange pain, though. Yes, she'd missed it and in that moment, there was an almost euphoric sense of returning to a completely different home. But at the same time, she knew there were people within these walls who had assumed she was guilty—that she'd helped Samson kill his first several victims and had only pretended to be diligently hunting him down. It would be interesting, she thought, to see how many of those people would seek her out to apologize.

She tucked this bit of resentment away, determined not to let it eat at her. It would be difficult when she saw her Assistant Director face to face, of course. She'd never felt that AD Mueller had done enough to make sure she didn't go to trial or to even make sure she stayed out of prison.

She headed for the front desk, feeling a bit like an impostor. She was dressed in the only sensible clothes she'd found still residing in her closet, having done a single load of laundry the night before. The button-down shirt didn't fit as well thanks to her well-toned shoulders, and she didn't miss the slacks at all during her time behind bars. But she thought she looked professional enough.

She didn't recognize the woman who was stationed there. This didn't surprise Morgan at all; she'd been gone for ten years. Surely, lots of personnel had changed. The girl at the front was young, no older than twenty-five if Morgan had to guess.

"Hello," the young woman said. "How can I help you?"

"Yes, I'm here to see…"

But she wasn't sure how to finish it. Should she ask to speak with her old director? Assistant Director Mueller was probably still here. If he wasn't, Derik would have surely mentioned it during his brief visit yesterday. But did she really want to see Mueller right away? They'd gotten along fine for the most part, but he could be a hard-ass.

"I have an appointment with Special Agent Derik Greene," she said.

"Of course," the receptionist said, picking up the landline phone. "Your name, please?"

"Morgan Cross."

She saw no look of shock or recognition on the woman's face as she punched in Derik's extension. Morgan took this as a good sign. If a panel had been assembled regarding her getting to work on a case concerning the Seven Signs Killer, it was being kept private. That was good. The last thing she wanted was for a dramatic return, all eyes on her. Especially when about half of the agents had doubted her innocence when she'd been arrested.

Derik showed up just two minutes later. Morgan was not ashamed to admit that she was pleased to see the look of shock on his face.

"I really wasn't sure if you'd come or not," he said.

Morgan smiled wryly. "I wasn't sure either."

Derik nodded, his eyes scanning her over. "You look different today. Did you get a good night's sleep?"

"Sure." She wasn't certain how to respond to the small talk. Derik had never resorted to such measures before. It didn't seem like him at all. It made her wonder what the last ten years had been like for him. What things had happened to him to cause such a change?

"You showed up at the perfect time," he said as they took a flight of stairs to the second floor. "The panel is assembled right now. A lead came through this morning. We just confirmed it about half an hour ago."

"And who is on this panel?"

"AD Mueller, AD Yen, Special Agent Whitmore, and me."

"Whitmore?" she asked. She didn't recognize the name.

"He came in about two years ago. A transfer from the Dallas office."

"Does he know the Seven Signs case well?"

"Well enough, but he's a bit of a savant about religious-themed murders. Still, we know we need your expertise on this. The new team we've assembled hasn't been able to make any headway. We need someone who knows this killer inside and out. Whitmore is actually a little excited to meet you."

"Did he think I was innocent when it all went down?" She hated how bitter the question sounded, but it was already out before she regretted saying it.

"I'm not sure. If I'm being honest, I've not been able to bring myself to ask him. I don't know if I want to know the answer. Just...remember he wasn't here at the time it went down, and he doesn't know you at all."

They came to the top of the stairs and Morgan nearly grew dizzy from the assault of emotion. She followed Derik down the familiar hallways, the memories flooding back as they walked. She tried not to let it affect her, but it was difficult. It was like walking through a museum of her past.

Derik led her to a conference room, where several other agents were waiting. She'd been in the room many times in the past, but it looked different now. The table was new, the chairs were different, and there were now three dry erase boards on the wall as opposed to the single dingy one she'd once used.

Each member of the group looked up as Morgan entered. She could feel their eyes on her and tried not to let it get to her.

Her own eyes did linger on Assistant Director Mueller for a moment. He'd aged considerably in the last ten years. He'd grown a beard that had gone mostly gray, and his widow's peak was much more pronounced. He smiled at her, and she worried that he was about to even get to his feet.

She simply nodded to him. She was glad to see him, she supposed, but she was also still slightly angry that they'd expected her to come running right away when they called, even if it was just one single day after being released from prison.

For a sentence she may have been able to avoid had the bureau fought a little harder for her.

She also recognized AD Yen. She'd never worked closely with him but knew his face. He was about fifty, clean-shaven, and didn't seem at all affected by her presence.

"Agent Cross," AD Yen said.

"Nope. Just Morgan. I don't know about the agent part yet."

"But...you came," Mueller said.

"I did. I came because my old partner told me Samson is back. I'm here because none of you apparently think this can be done without me."

Mueller and Derik both looked taken aback. Derik had taken a seat at the table, but Morgan remained standing. She liked that they seemed

19

to not know how to handle her now. She'd never been this forward and rough in the past.

"You...you've seen the file?" Mueller asked.

"I have. Agent Greene brought it over to my house yesterday. I've looked through it. The only thing new I saw was the drowning deaths at Kisanthum River."

"I also told her we had a new lead that just came in," Derik pointed out.

"He did," Morgan said, still opting not to sit. "What's the lead?"

Mueller eyed her for a moment and then shrugged. Apparently, he was willing to roll with her new attitude. The ease in which he made this decision told Morgan all she needed to know: he'd not been expecting her to show up and because she was here now, he wasn't about to make things harder than they had to be. She actually respected him for this.

"A man showed up in two surveillance cameras at two o'clock in the morning on the day the bodies were discovered on the banks," Mueller said.

"The cameras are positioned at the parking lot near the canoe rentals and then again over near the pavilions you can rent for parties," Derik said.

"Do we know who he is?" she asked.

"Not yet," AD Yen said, opening up a folder and sliding a photo across the table to Morgan. "But we do have a clear image of his face."

Morgan picked up the photo and examined it closely. It was a man in his mid-thirties, with short, dark hair and a sharp jawline. He looked like an average guy, but something about his expression made her uneasy. It was almost like he was smirking at the camera.

"So no ID yet?" Morgan asked.

"No," Derik said. "But we're running facial recognition software on him now. We'll know soon enough."

Morgan nodded, setting down the photo. "What about the victims? Anything new on them?"

"We've been able to identify all the victims," AD Yen said. "We've been in touch with their families, but none of them have any leads for us. We're still trying to piece together any connections they might have had."

Morgan nodded, feeling a familiar sense of frustration. This was the same problem they'd had ten years ago. The Seven Signs Killer was careful. He didn't leave any evidence behind, and he didn't seem to have any clear motive for his killings.

"There's one more thing," Mueller said. "Each victim had a piece of paper in their mouth. The killer made sure it stayed in their mouths because their mouths were taped shut when he put them in the river."

"What was on the paper?"

"A reference to scripture," Derik said. "Mark 6:45–53. It's the story of Jesus walking on water."

"He never left clues like that before," Morgan said. "I mean, he left his vague letters, but never actually pointing to scripture, right?"

"Right. We think he did it this time so we'd make no mistake it was him," Yen said. "He wanted us to know he was picking back up."

"You do know that he stopped when you went away, right?" Agent Whitmore said.

"Went away?" Morgan asked, angry. "I did a little more than 'went away.'" Looking away from Whitmore, she went on. "Okay, so we have a new lead and a new symbol. "What's the plan from here?"

"We want you to lead this investigation," Mueller said.

"Me? Why?"

"Because you're the only one who's ever been close to catching the Seven Signs Killer," Mueller said. "You know him better than anyone else in this bureau."

"You understand I just got out of prison, right? After ten years?"

"Yes. And we don't think it's a coincidence that he stopped when you were put in prison and picked back up just three days before you were released. For whatever reason, he wants you to come for him."

There was an obvious question to be asked here. But even as the question formed in her mind, she knew the answer.

The question: *So do we just give the maniac exactly what he wants?*

The answer wasn't quite as simple. Yes…they had to give him what he wanted. If they wanted to know why he was doing this and to figure out how to stop him from killing even more people, there had to be a hunt. So, yes…he was calling her out and she was going to him. It felt a bit careless and rash.

But was there really any other way to get it done?

Morgan let out a sigh. She knew Mueller was right. She was the only one who had ever come close to catching him. But that was ten years ago. She'd stayed in shape in prison, but…well, she was a different person now.

"Morgan?" Mueller said. "This is urgent. What do you say?"

"I say I need to know who to talk to about that facial recognition software. And…what do I need to do to get a temporary badge and gun?"

Mueller looked uncomfortable at the very mention of this, but Morgan was a bit relieved to notice that Derik was smiling.

CHAPTER FOUR

The facial recognition software provided results forty minutes later. In that time, Morgan had managed to secure a temporary badge, a standard bureau-issued Glock, and a complete file of all of the Seven Signs Killer's activities from ten years ago.

Morgan felt as if she'd been swept up in a whirlwind. Less than twelve hours ago, none of this had been on her radar. She'd been mostly concerned with just trying to reclaim her footing in the real world. She still had a house that needed to be properly cleaned and organized. She had a dog that she needed to care for and spend time with.

But somehow, here she was, back in the one single element of her life that had been responsible for putting her in prison in the first place. Things were a bit different, of course. She'd been gone for a decade, after all; she had no office of her own, so she found herself sitting in a small unoccupied conference room, quickly signing several papers that made it lawful and official to head back out.

"I still can't believe they're just giving you a gun."

She looked up and saw Derik standing in the doorway. Much like his visit to her house yesterday, he looked both elated to see her but nervous, too.

"They didn't just give it to me," she said. "Do you see this ridiculous stack of papers?"

"I do. And Mueller just told me to tell you to stop. He's got the important one signed…the ones that give you permission to go out as a temporary agent."

She tossed the pen down and looked up at Derik, truly taking him in for the first time today. "And I assume you'll be accompanying me?"

He nodded and smiled. "Just like old times."

"Which means I'll be doing all the driving?"

"Nope. I don't think you've signed that piece of paper yet. Here or at the DMV from what I gather."

She didn't know if he was being serious or not, but she followed him out of the room anyway. As she trailed behind him on the way to the small garage on the northern rim of the field office property, the sights and turns of the hallways all pulled nostalgia out of her. Some were pleasant, but there were a few landmarks along the course of the building that felt as if that same nostalgia was being torn at with hooks.

She passed by the hallway that led to the interrogation rooms—four distinct, small rooms where she'd spent a great deal of time. While interrogation wasn't by any means what she thought of as her sweet spot, she knew she was good at it. She was *so* good at it that she would be called in for cases that weren't even hers. Some other agent would simply give her a case file to study and then, a few hours later, she'd go in and mentally break the suspect down.

She felt a little sting of memory as they passed by the small break room near the back of the building, where, in the early hours of morning after closing a case regarding the kidnapping of three siblings, she and Derik had shared a kiss. It had been brief but passionate…and they'd never kissed again. In fact, they'd never even mentioned that one kiss.

And that had been fine with her. She hadn't been interested in a relationship with anyone back then…let alone the married man she was partnered with at work.

Passing by all of this was all too weird, and Morgan started to wonder if she'd made a mistake by coming back so soon. Memories were swarming at her like confused, angry bees and she was already tired of feeling the stings. Still, she remained quiet as she and Derik got a car from the bureau lot.

"So what do you know about the suspect?" Morgan asked as Derik pulled out of the lot. "I'm still trying to wrap my head around how quickly we got results back from the software. Things have changed a lot in ten years."

"His name's Marcus Black," Derik said. "No known criminal history, standard employment record, no social media presence. Seems like mostly a good boy."

"Any idea why he was by the river that night?"

"Nope. That's what we need to find out. You saw that in the information we got back, we have his home and work addresses, right?"

"Yeah."

"I figured we'd head to his workplace first, being a Wednesday morning. Cape Lumber Supplies."

"Yeah, agreed."

"And we do have one other lead," Derik continued. "One of the victims was a nurse at the same hospital where Black was treated for a broken arm about eight months ago."

"But no other direct connections between the victims?"

"No. We're still cross-referencing all of their data, but so far we haven't found any clear connections. They all come from different backgrounds and have different lifestyles."

Morgan nodded. "At some point, I want to talk to the families of the victims. Maybe they can shed some light on any connections they might have had to Black."

Derik looked at her skeptically. "Do you think it's him? Do you think Marcus Black might be the so-called Samson? That he might be the Seven Signs Killer?"

She knew what she thought but didn't want to speak it out loud. What she was thinking was that if this was indeed the guy, it seemed very strange that they'd find him now, one day after she'd been released from prison. She also knew there were any number of reasons a random man might be out along the river at night, most having to do with drugs or sexual situations.

She'd seen suspects like this come and go while she'd been on the case before. Some had been incredibly promising and on two occasions, she'd been certain they'd found Samson. But the evidence would always point in another direction, leaving her and Derik disappointed and with empty hands.

***

The rest of the drive was spent in silence, both of them lost in their own thoughts. Morgan couldn't help but feel a sense of déjà vu. She was essentially back in the same car, with the same partner, chasing after the same killer.

At the same time, there was a feeling of exhilaration to be in a car again. Even if there wasn't a case somewhere out there ahead of them, the feeling of moving forward so quickly with a set of wheels beneath her was more rewarding than she'd expected. Driving or even being the passenger in a car was not something she'd thought she'd come out of prison with a new appreciation for…but here she was, feeling like a kid out for a joy ride.

Unsurprisingly, it brought up another memory of her father. It hit her like a brick right to the side of the head, visions of him taking her about an hour outside of the city to an old stretch of abandoned farmland. He'd taught her to drive a stick shift at the age of thirteen, in an old Chevy truck.

She remembered the roads, the fields, the way the transmission had clunked and screeched at her. Before she knew what was happening, Morgan felt the memory encompass her and she saw every detail clearly.

She was back in that old Chevy truck, sitting next to her father. The sun was setting, casting a warm orange glow over everything. Morgan could feel the rough texture of the steering wheel beneath her fingers, and the scent of gasoline and oil filling her nose. She could feel the way her father's rough hands had steadied hers on the wheel, the way he'd barked out instructions as she'd shifted gears for the first time. It had been a bonding moment for them, one of many.

Her father was patient with her, guiding her through each step of the process. And when she finally got the hang of it, he'd grinned at her proudly.

"You okay?"

Derik's voice pulled her out of the memory, and she was rather glad for it. Now was not the time to start getting overly emotional.

Morgan nodded. "Yeah, just lost in thought."

"You want to talk about it?"

Morgan shook her head. "No, it's nothing. Just a memory from a long time ago."

She could tell that he wanted to ask her more about it, but he kept quiet. It was a startling reminder of just how well Derik knew her. He knew when to push but, more importantly, when not to.

They arrived at Cape Lumber Supplies at just after eleven. It was a sizable privately owned store on the eastern edge of the city, located in a small strip of stores and shops. When Derik parked and they got out of the car, Morgan felt another of those weird familiar pangs. It was like she hadn't been away for more than a week, but at the same time, she felt like a ghost haunting a world she could barely remember. She supposed it would be very different if she'd been working alongside anyone other than Derik.

Actually, had it been anyone other than Derik, she doubted she would have come back so soon. If at all.

They walked in through a large set of double sliding doors. The store was one large warehouse of sorts, the back half occupied by enormous shelves with stacks upon stacks of lumber. The smell was pleasant, something like sawdust and a woodsy aroma. The front of the place consisted of three different check-out areas that looked quite different from any other store Morgan had ever been to. She assumed all of the actual purchasing of goods took place in the back.

They headed for one of these check-out kiosks, and Morgan approached a man who looked to be in his early fifties. He greeted them warmly but the look he gave them made it clear that they weren't the usual sort that came into their store.

"Can I help you folks?" he asked.

"We need to speak with Marcus Black," Derik said. "Is he in today?"

Morgan noticed how quickly Derik spoke up. He was making no effort to hide the fact that for now, he expected her to keep a backseat position. She was only here for her familiarity and expertise...and because it seemed that for some unknown reason, the Seven Signs Killer felt that the two of them were connected. To stop killing when she was arrested and to start up again just three days before she was released—they both knew there was no coincidence there.

"He is," the man said. "You'll find him back in aisle six, sawing up some two-by-fours, I think."

They gave their thanks and made their way back through the maze-like structure of tall shelves. As they neared aisle 6, Morgan could hear the buzzing of a saw. It grew louder as they came to the aisle and started down it. At the far end, easily thirty yards away, she could see a man hunched over a large pneumatic saw, feeding a pack of cedar through it.

For safety, they waited until the man, presumably Marcus Black, cleared the plank from the saw platform. The unused end clattered to the floor as Black stacked the newly cut two-by-four to the right. He had a nice pile going, stacked nearly three feet high.

"Excuse me," Derik said. "Marcus Black?"

The man turned around, his eyes wide with surprise behind the protective glasses. The resemblance to the picture they had from the security camera footage was dead-on. It was without a doubt the same man.

"Yeah, that's me. Who're you?"

"Special Agents Greene and Cross, FBI," he said, making quick work of flashing his badge.

"Okay...um, how can I help you?"

"We have your face on security footage from a parking lot just off the banks of the Kisanthum River four nights ago. Would you deny being there if pressed?"

"No," he said with a slight tremor of fear in his voice. "I was there."

"Why?" Morgan asked.

Black's eyes darted between the two agents, a nervous sweat breaking out on his forehead. He swallowed hard before finally speaking. "I…I like to go there to think. It's a quiet place, you know?"

"That late at night?"

"That's when it's quiet. I like the sounds, you know? Crickets, frogs."

You said you went there to think. What were you thinking about that night?"

Black hesitated before answering. "Just…life, I guess. I had a lot on my mind."

"Can you be more specific?" Derik asked, leaning in a little closer.

Black took a step back, his eyes darting around nervously. "I don't know, man. Just stuff. Work, bills, that kind of thing." He was getting agitated and, Morgan thought, a bit defensive.

Plus, Morgan could tell he was lying. There was something in the way he avoided eye contact, in the way he fidgeted with his hands, that told her he was hiding something. She decided to go in for a more direct approach.

"Mr. Black, several hours after your face appeared on that footage, four people were found dead on the banks. They'd been drowned. And upon doing background checks on them, we determined that one was a nurse at the hospital where you were treated for a broken arm a few months ago."

"What? Four…dead?"

"Yes." She was quite certain he was still lying, but he did seem shocked. "What can you tell us about that?"

"Nothing…nothing, I swear."

He was trying to take a few steps back and his face was setting quite hard. He was angry now. And as she watched him, his right hand slowly dropped to the side, where a cracked two-by-four was propped against the wall.

"We need you to come with us," Derik said. "We'll have a chat down at the office and—"

"No," Black said. There was a moment of hesitation and then, as if he'd just suddenly made the decision to do so, he brought the cracked two-by-four up.

It caught Derik by surprise. He brought his arm up, but Morgan knew it would be too late to block the board from slamming into the side of his head. And even if he did keep it from hitting his head, the blow would probably crack his wrist apart.

Thinking quickly and acting reflexively, Morgan doled out a fast and hard right-handed jab. She aimed low, blasting Black in the ribs. The blow caused him to stumble and release the board before it hit Derik's head. It fell, barely striking Derik in the leg.

Black wheeled around in pain and surprise. He opened his mouth in an angry sneer, intending to say something. But Morgan didn't give him the chance. She blasted that same right-handed jab out, this time clipping him in the jaw.

She regretted it the moment she'd made contact. Even after a decade in prison where she'd somehow only managed to participate in three fights, she knew this was too much, that this was over the line.

"Christ, Morgan…" Derik said. "Take it easy."

She took a guilty step back as Black fell back, his eyes dreamy and almost closing. When he fell the side of his head struck the platform of the saw and he went out like a light.

Morgan was shocked at just how quickly she'd resorted to violence. But then again, it was something she'd learned in prison…something she'd quickly had to adapt to. And after just three visible fights among the inmates those first two years, she'd been left alone.

Plus, she saw a bit of awe in Derik's eyes as he looked back and forth between her and Marcus Black. And even as he leaned down to help the man to his feet and apply handcuffs, Morgan was pretty sure he was biting back a smile. Yes, he was absolutely worried about what she'd done, but she saw the smirk hiding in his worry, too.

Morgan wasn't quite as entertained, though. Those punches had come out of nowhere and she knew the one to his ribs had been much harder than she anticipated. If she was going to truly make a go of helping the bureau bring in the Seven Signs Killer, she was going to have to get herself under control.

"You good?" Derik asked as he eyed her with skepticism.

"Yeah," she said, looking at her hands as if she didn't quite trust them. "Sorry…I just…"

But she didn't know how to finish the statement. All she could do was follow Derik out of the store as he escorted a handcuffed Marcus Black to the front door.

CHAPTER FIVE

He'd kept up with news of Morgan Cross. He'd been vigilant about it, keeping up with the memos and news stories.

His man on the inside had told him when she was getting out of prison, and he'd wanted to make sure she was welcomed back to the world of the free warmly.

So he'd started again just a few days before her release. And it felt so good...like he'd never stopped. His work was coming to completion, and he had so much inspiration and energy stored up from the past ten years that he had no doubt it was going to end with the kind of bang people would be talking about for decades.

It almost made it worth the ten-year pause.

Not that he was doing it for the attention. No...he was doing it because the world needed to be woken up. They needed to see their flaws and live in fear of their wretched sinful nature.

The Seven Signs were such a pure picture of what life could be. Paradise. A place of miracles and wonders. He was simply trying to help them see that.

And next was the healing of the blind man. In a way, Morgan Cross's time away had helped him prepare for this. Because blind people tended to have so much assistance, he'd had to plan very carefully for this sign. It had taken years to find the right candidate and then several months of very careful stakeouts and stalking to get the soon-to-be victim's schedule just right.

He was watching the blind man now while sitting on the steps of a neighboring building, pretending to read a book. He watched as the blind man stepped out of an Uber in front of his apartment building. He used his cane to tap his way to the ramp that bypassed the stairs of the apartment building. He really was a very brave and adept man.

It was actually a shame he had to die.

He checked his watch. The blind man's helper would be there in ten minutes, and then leave an hour later. From there, he'd have a twelve-hour window before a woman he thought was the man's mother would come by.

And that was plenty of time to do what needed to be done. He could take his time with it. He could make it special.

He hoped Morgan Cross would appreciate it.

He also hoped that in the end, whichever way this all came to a close, she'd be able to appreciate how he'd come to frame her...how *she* had gone to prison while he'd gone free.

It made him giddy with excitement...and more anxious than ever to kill again.

He could hardly wait.

CHAPTER SIX

As Morgan and Derik entered the field office through the back entrance, Mueller was waiting for them. He was standing with his back propped against the wall directly at the intersection that led to the interrogation rooms. And he did not look happy.

"I need an explanation," he said. His eyes were locked directly on Morgan. He barely even registered that they had a suspect in custody.

"For what, sir?"

Mueller rolled his eyes. "I got a call from Cape Lumber Supplies. They say you roughed this man up."

"Damn right she did," Marcus Black spat.

Mueller then looked to Derik, as if hoping for a logical answer. Before he could say anything, Morgan answered. She hated to feel that Derik was her babysitter, that he was on the verge of trying to cover for her violent outburst.

"I lost control," she said simply. "I…I lost control of myself, plain and simple."

Mueller stared at her for a long moment before nodding slowly. "And you think that's acceptable behavior for a federal agent?"

"No," Morgan said. "I don't."

Mueller looked back to Derik and gestured toward the interrogation rooms. "Agent Greene, go ahead and take your suspect to interrogation."

It looked like Derik wanted to argue about this, but decided against it. He gave Black a small nudge as they made their way past Mueller and down the hallway.

"This is partly on me," Mueller said. "I don't know what the hell I was thinking…what we were thinking."

"It was one slip-up," Morgan argued

"One slip-up after you've only been back in the field for an hour and a half. Morgan…we need you on this case. I'm not dumb enough to ignore that. But right now, in the wake of the call I just got, I need you to go home."

"Now?"

"Yes."

"For how long?"

He thought about it for a moment and said: "At least the rest of the day. And I know you can't drive yet...so I've already called an Uber for you. It's out front, waiting."

Morgan opened her mouth to protest, but Mueller held up a hand. "It's not up for discussion. Once things are settled back in interrogation, we'll FaceTime you. But for now...you can't be here."

She turned and walked away, hurrying down the hallway to the left before she said something she knew she'd regret. And when she finally made her way outside, her ride was waiting for her, just as Mueller had said.

When she got into the back seat, she slammed the door so hard the driver gave her a worried look.

***

Even through the screen of the iPad, Director Mueller looked beaten. Morgan didn't think he looked mad, though. Maybe disappointed. As she sat on her stale, musty couch, she waited for him to say something. She assumed they would terminate their temporary agreement, coming to the decision that it had been a bad idea from the start.

If so, Morgan would wholeheartedly agree.

"Well, the good news is that Black has signed papers that indicate he won't be pressing charges," Mueller finally said.

"Oh. Well, that's good."

"Cross, what were you thinking?"

This again, she thought. But she also knew he was trying to keep appearances...that this call would go down on public record in regards to the case. He had to play the part of director. He had to be a hard-ass.

"Honestly, sir, I wasn't. It just happened. I'm sure you understand that I'm a bit rusty. And my mind is still in tune with living in prison, among people I never trusted."

"I get that."

She watched him wrestle with what to do. She supposed he was wondering if he'd acted rashly when she and Derik had brought Marcus Black in, and he'd sent her home.

Based on what she'd just been told, Derik had filled the panel in on what had happened at the store, giving a blow-by-blow breakdown. No one on the panel was particularly happy, especially given the fact that it seemed that Marcus Black was not their man.

33

As she watched Mueller mulling over what needed to be done, Morgan couldn't help but wonder if she was about to be released from her contract or agreement, or whatever it was. Beyond that, she wondered if her slip-up from this morning might cost her any chance she'd ever had of returning to work with the Behavioral Analysis Unit at all.

"Let's cut to the chase, sir. What do you want from me? Do I need to sign some more papers to terminate this little experiment?"

"That would be the wise answer, yes. But we can't deny that this killer feels he has a connection of some kind to you."

"This killer? So it wasn't Black, correct?"

"Correct. There's more than enough evidence to support it. He has about five different alibis and four have already checked out."

"So what do you want me to do?" Morgan asked.

Mueller sighed and she could tell what he said next pained him. "We want you to stay on the case. We need your help because of your history with the killer. The truth of the matter is that no one blames you for how you reacted today. If anything, it's our fault. To expect you to just come back and step right back into this role…"

She knew what he was struggling with. She wondered if he'd come out and admit that they'd made a mistake when they arrested her. When they thought she'd actually been helping the Seven Signs Killer rather than trying to catch him.

But apparently, he wasn't ready to address that particular elephant in the room just yet.

"We know it's a lot to ask," he went on. "But we believe you have a unique perspective and set of skills that could be invaluable to us. For now, though…maybe you work the case from a less visible platform. You won't come into the office, and you'll only speak with suspects when it's absolutely crucial."

"So you're tying my hands."

"A bit, yes. But after the bullet we dodged with Black today, we have no choice."

A question rose to her lips…one she was hesitant to ask. "With all due respect, sir…what if I say no?"

"Then we'll do our best without you. But Cross…we both know you won't say no. What will you do? Watch from the sidelines as this psychopath finishes what he sees as his work?"

He'd called her bluff a little too quickly. She chuckled a bit as Skunk came over to her, leaping up on the couch. Lora had brought him over as soon as she'd gotten home. He seemed to already be making himself at home. Morgan hoped it was because he'd somehow managed to remember who she was.

"Fine," she said. "Keep me posted. I'll do what I can."

"Thanks, Cross. All updates and breaks in the case will come from Agent Greene."

There was no drawn-out goodbye. She simply ended the call and sighed, petting Skunk between the ears. And then, before she could allow her mind to focus on the conversation she'd just had with Mueller, she set her eyes to the living room. She still needed to clean, to organize. She needed to go to the grocery store, needed to straighten out the legalities and payments for a cellphone, internet service, and so on. She needed a laptop, maybe a new TV. She needed to sort out things with the bank and...

Or, she thought, *you can revisit those pills in the bathroom and not worry about any of this shit.*

No. She got to her feet before that train of thought could even leave the station. She would focus on getting the house straight, on doing everything she could to bring order and organization to a mind that had become angry and violent over the past ten years.

So, finding some old, dusty cleaning supplies in the barren laundry room, she began.

Morgan scrubbed and wiped at every surface in the living room until it shone. Skunk watched her, his head cocked to one side as if he was trying to understand what she was doing. She moved on to the kitchen, scrubbing the fridge and plugging it in, wiping down the counters. As she worked, she realized that cleaning was a form of therapy for her. It was something she could control, something she could fix.

But no amount of cleaning could fix the fact that there was a killer out there, a killer who had already taken nine lives—and that was based on only five of the signs. He was taking multiple lives per sign when he could, so there was never any telling how many would die when he attacked. He was clever and methodical...very careful and meticulous about what he did.

And now, she was being asked to work the case from the sidelines. It was frustrating, but she knew Mueller was right: she belonged on this case in any way she could get on.

As she scrubbed the sink, her eyes drifted over to the picture her father had left for her. She missed him terribly but hadn't yet grieved him properly. How could she, having been in prison. The idea that she'd never see him again seemed foreign and odd, something her mind simply could not fathom.

And it was that sense of despair (and roughly four hours of cleaning) that sent her to the shower as the day came to a close. She took her time, showering until the hot water started to run out, and then went to bed.

Skunk immediately curled up at her feet. Morgan had just enough time to notice, as she had last night, that the sheets smelled quite old and dusty. She added "wash the sheets" to her growing mental list of things to do but was asleep before she fully had time to process it.

Her sleep instantly threw her into a nightmare…or as instantly as sleep makes it seem.

She was swimming in a river and there were four people walking toward her. They were all dead, zombies walking on the water and laughing at her. She swam hard for the shore but as she drew closer to the banks, she saw that the only thing waiting for her was a prison cell. Her father waited there, also dead. He was waving to her, as if he hadn't seen her in forever, and when she waved back it was only then that she realized he wasn't waving to her at all. He was waving to the dead people on the water.

"You're going to fail again," he said.

She was torn out of the nightmare by the ringing of her phone. She grabbed it right away because it was an anchor to the real world, proof that the nightmare wasn't real. She took a moment to collect her breath, still seeing those zombies on the water.

"Yeah? Hello?"

"Hey, Morgan. It's Derik…sorry to call so early."

How early was it? she wondered. She hadn't even checked the time on the phone when she answered it and there was no bedside clock.

"What time is it?"

"A bit past five in the morning. Look…can you be ready in twenty minutes?"

"Yeah. Why?"

"Because the Seven Signs Killer has just fulfilled the sixth sign."

CHAPTER SEVEN

When Morgan stepped into the apartment, she was horrified at just how clearly she could smell the freshly spilled blood. She of course hadn't stepped foot in a crime scene in years, so maybe her senses had forgotten what it was like. Back in the day, she'd been used to it…the scent like copper and, underneath, something almost like sweat. It wasn't too dissimilar from getting used to the smell of your own house.

But her body had adjusted to the smells of prison cells and body odor, of pungent cleaning supplies and dust. The smell of the victim's fresh blood was almost sickening.

She did her best to stay in control as she and Derik stepped into the apartment. There were three people already there; two were uniformed cops, standing in the large room that served as an adjoined kitchen and living area, and the other was a man of about thirty-five or so. He was sitting on the couch, his hands in his head, stifling small cries.

As one of the cops came over—the other busy with trying to speak to and comfort the man on the couch—Morgan took a moment to closely study the body of the victim. It was a male, dressed in a very basic suit. He was lying face down on his kitchen floor, a pool of blood surrounding his head like a halo. It was hard to tell with his back to them, but Morgan was quite sure he'd been struck or cut on the head.

Roughly three feet away from the blood was a single scrap of paper. The number 6 had been written on it in red marker.

"What do we have here?" Derik asked.

The cop, a grizzled-looking man of middle age, looked down at the victim with a frown. "Victor Rhyman. Forty-one years of age. Discovered forty minutes ago by the gentleman on the couch."

"At such an early hour?" Morgan asked.

"Yes. Mr. Rhyman was blind, and—"

"And I'm a part-time caretaker," the man on the couch said, looking up but trying to keep his eyes away from the body.

"Your name?" Derik asked.

"Lee Case."

As Morgan slowly made her way over to Lee Case, she heard Derik whisper to the officer. "We're good here."

The other officer must have heard this because they got up from the couch and followed the other officer into the kitchen, near the door.

"Mr. Case," Morgan said, "can you walk us through the moment you discovered the body?"

Lee shuddered and looked up at Morgan, his eyes filled with tears. "I...I came in to check on Mr. Rhyman like I usually do. He was blind and needed help with a few things around the apartment. When I walked in, I found him lying there like that. I didn't know what to do, so I called 911."

Morgan nodded understandingly. "And before that, did you hear anything unusual or see anyone suspicious around the building?"

Case shook his head. "No, I didn't. I just came in and found him like that."

Morgan could tell he was telling the truth. She turned to Derik and saw and look of understanding in his eyes as well. They were both quite certain Lee Case had nothing to do with the murder.

"How long have you been working with him?" Morgan asked.

"About three years."

"And did he have any enemies? Maybe even people he was scared of?"

Lee shook his head. "No...nothing like that."

"When you arrived this morning, was the door opened or closed?"

"It was closed, but unlocked. And I knew then that something was wrong. Mr. Rhyman always makes sure to lock his doors. He's actually a bit compulsive about it."

As Morgan considered this, Derik turned to the officers. "We'll need to take a closer look around the rest of the building. Check for any signs of forced entry or anything else that might give us a lead."

Morgan's mind was already racing, trying to piece together the clues. The number 6 on the paper was simple enough. It was the killer's card...a way for him to make certain they knew this was his responsibility...that he had done this. He'd left similar scraps for Victims 1, 2, and 4.

And she'd studied the Seven Signs enough during the original case to understand the significance of Rhyman being blind. In the Bible, in the Book of John to be exact, Jesus had healed a man who had been blind from birth. In the back of her mind, Morgan felt foolish for not expecting this—the murder of a blind man. But in her mind, she'd always assumed the killer would have taken the victim's eyes or stabbed them in their eyes...something like that.

But he'd been very literal this time. He was getting to the end of his work now. He wasn't messing around.

"Cross, you good?" Derik asked.

She nodded. "You go on with the officers. I want to look the body over. Maybe look around the place. Mr. Case…maybe you should head out with them, too."

As Lee got to his feet, Derik eyed her skeptically but said nothing. He stepped forward and escorted Lee Case around the body. Derik then led Lee and the officers out through the door. He closed it slowly on his way out, leaving Morgan alone with the body.

She wouldn't dare turn it over or touch the body until forensics arrived. She knew better than that from the trouble that had gone down ten years ago…the trouble that had landed her in jail for a decade. So instead, she did a slow scan of the living room and kitchen.

The apartment was tidy, maybe even a little too tidy, with everything in its place. There was no sign of a struggle or disruption. No overturned furniture or broken items. It was as if someone had just walked in, killed the victim, and walked out.

Morgan took a closer look at the scrap of paper with the number 6 on it. She knew that they'd find no fingerprints on it, just like the other scraps from ten years ago. Samson was careful. He'd thought things out. And now, ten years later, he seemed to not have missed a step.

She continued her search, moving toward the door that led to the bedroom. As she stepped inside, she paused for a moment, taking in the room. It was just as neat as the rest of the apartment, with the bed made up and the sheets neatly tucked in.

But something caught her eye…something that seemed strange in the bedroom of a blind man.

A well-used keyboard sat in the corner. Sitting on a stand with a small bench in front of it, the keyboard was a bulky thing, the sort used for electronic artists rather than students that were just learning. To the right, on a small bookshelf, were a few books. She knelt down and studied them, finding with no surprise that they were all in Braille. Stuffed in among some of the books were two flyers.

She plucked them both out and saw that they were handouts from Heron Methodist Church. It was apparently a very small church because the handout was only one page…front and back. She scanned it and found Victor Rhyman's name on it. He was listed as "organ and music."

She considered this for a moment. She knew that a few of the earlier victims had been heavily involved in church. But that had been

39

ten years ago. Certainly finding connections and links between the victims now would be difficult…if not damn near impossible.

She set the handouts on the floor and stared at the keyboard. She imagined Rhyman sitting on the bench, learning songs for church despite his disadvantage. Something about it, and knowing that he was currently lying dead in a pool of his own blood out in the kitchen, made her feel helpless. It made her feel defeated and lost.

It reminded her of what she'd nearly done that first night back at her house. It made her think of the pills, of an easy way out, of…

A knock on the door broke the image apart. She exited the bedroom and made her way across the living room, then sidestepped the body in the kitchen to answer the front door. There were two forensics members on the other side. One was a man and the other a woman, both in their late twenties.

Morgan stepped back to let them work, and then stepped out of the apartment. She took a deep breath of fresh air out in the hallway, trying to clear her mind. She pulled out her phone and dialed Derik.

It started to ring, and she thought of the pills again. She thought of a warm bath and a razor.

Jesus, she thought. *What is this? What's wrong with me…?*

She thought the answer was clear. She'd been in prison for ten years and within just two days of being released she was back on the very same case that had put her there.

"Yeah?" Derik's voice answered in her ear.

"I got a small nugget of information," she said. "It seems Rhyman played the organ at a local Methodist church."

"Seems like a connection to at least a few others, huh?"

"Yeah, that's what I'm thinking. You ready to head to the station?"

He hesitated for a moment and then, with maybe a bit too much sincerity in his voice for Morgan's liking, he said, "Yes, but are you?"

Morgan sighed and bit back the vile retort that came to her tongue. In the end, she only said, "I'll meet you downstairs."

With that, she left the body of Victor Rhyman to forensics, hoping there might still be a few viable connections lingering among the victims even after a decade away.

CHAPTER EIGHT

Morgan wasn't sure what she'd been expecting when she logged onto the precinct's database, but it certainly hadn't been an amplified depression. Everything about it was different beyond the log-in screen. She also discovered that because of her prolonged absence and guilty verdict, she'd been removed from network access anyway.

She was rather delighted to find that this angered Derik almost as much as it angered her.

"You'd think," he said, plopping himself down in his office chair, "that they'd make sure this crap was straightened out before asking you to rush back into this damned case."

"No access to the database, no office...I'm not feeling too good about my chances of coming back full-time after this case."

Derik was pulling a spare chair over. It was one he kept in the corner, littered with books and three different jackets. He removed the books and positioned the chair beside his, so that it was facing his laptop. He then looked at her with a curious smile.

"Do you think you'd come back full-time?"

"I don't know. It depends."

"On what?"

Morgan shrugged. "I don't know that either. So...show me this newfangled database system."

He showed her the ins and outs of the new system as they hunted down connections and leads from the previous victims that might somehow tie into the most recent killings. As he did, Morgan started to feel the frustration all over again. They knew the murders were linked because the Seven Signs Killer was pointing it out to them. And because of the stories of the Seven Signs in the Bible, they had at least some indication of what the murders would look like.

So how in the hell had this guy evaded them for so long?

"Tell me," Derik said about half an hour later as he printed out the backgrounds of six different potential suspects. Some were being recycled from their first batch of interviews and interrogations from a decade ago, but there were some new names, too. Honestly, none of it felt solid to Morgan.

"Tell you what?"

"If we don't catch this guy and he gets his tenth victim…or however many he'd able to take out with his next little sign. Do you think he'll just disappear? Do you think he'll consider his work done?"

Morgan leaned back in her chair, considering Derik's question. She knew it was a possibility. Some serial killers stopped after reaching a specific number of victims or once they felt they had accomplished their "mission." Or because they were afraid they were on the brink of being caught.

But the Seven Signs Killer didn't strike her as someone who would just disappear. Even if he carried out his sick "seven signs," maybe he'd find some other religious symbol or account to inspire him. He seemed to take pride in getting the better of them, so she doubted he'd be able to simply stop.

"I don't think so," she said finally. "This guy is too meticulous, too calculated. He's been planning this for years. I don't think he'd just stop after reaching the seventh sign. He'll find a new way to continue his sick game."

Derik nodded, looking serious. "Yeah, that's how I feel. While you were in prison and he went quiet…we all thought he'd just stopped, you know? That what happened to you might have felt like it had hit too close to him."

"You mean for those of you who thought I was innocent?" she asked with just a bit of bite in her tone.

"Yeah…" He nearly fell quiet here, and Morgan could sense him wrestling with something. Finally, he turned to her and said: "You know, you have to stop pretending that everyone thought you were guilty. I never did. There are several others that were pissed when you went to prison, too. I can't even imagine what you're dealing with right now, or what the past ten years have been like…but you have to drop the grudge against me."

"Drop it? Derik, tell me…have you ever lost *ten years* of your life because everyone you worked with and respected thought you were responsible for the murders of several people?"

"Of course I haven't. You know I—"

"Then maybe think twice before you say something that stupid again."

Before he had a chance to respond, Morgan got up from the chair, grabbed the printouts from the printer in the corner, and left the room. She went to the front lobby and sat quietly, poring over the files. She knew right away that she'd reacted too harshly—that if there had been anyone at all on her side through her entire ordeal ten years ago and during the sentence itself, it had been Derik.

But it was too early to apologize, anyway. She knew Derik was a prideful man and they both just needed to sit in the tension of what had happened. As she looked at the files, she noted that a few people coming in and out of the precinct looked at her with great interest. She figured the rumors of her return had made it all the way through the building by now…as had the resurgence of the Seven Signs Killer.

But she shrugged it off, keeping her attention on the files. She had come to the final one about twenty minutes later when someone approached quickly from the hallway behind her.

"Morgan?"

It was Derik. He looked angry, but there was also a bit of excitement in his eyes.

"Yeah?"

He handed her the folder in his hand with as much professionalism as he could manage. "I think I found a hit. A guy named Andy Feeney. He was a priest at the church our fourth victim attended ten years ago. And it just so happens that he was excommunicated right around the time you were arrested. I'm talking within a few weeks. And do you want to guess when his excommunication was overturned and he returned to his position at the church?"

"When?"

"Last week. Just as the murders started again. Just before you returned home."

"Do you know where he is right now?"

"No, but I have a home address and an address for the church."

"Sounds good. And Derik, listen, what I said earlier…"

"Don't tell me you didn't mean it. You did mean it. And I sort of deserved it. The absolute iron will you must have to jump right back into this…I can't imagine it."

"I just want to stop this bastard," she said, tears of rage coming to her eyes. "I…I have to. I have to stop him to make these last ten years mean something."

Before he could say anything, she handed the folder back without even looking at it. He took it, saying, "Come on, then. Let's go find a priest."

"What about the restrictions Mueller placed on me? I'm not exactly able to come and go as I please, remember?"

"We'll have to be sneaky about it," he said finally. "I can't operate with my hands tied, and neither can you. Mueller knows that. Also…I

43

think when it all boils down, he's on your side. I think he's just trying to put on a strong face for the rest of the panel."

"You're sure about this?"

He smiled at her and when he locked eyes with her, she was reminded of that fleeting kiss in the break room nearly eleven years ago. It then occurred to her that ten years had taken a lot more from her than she realized...including the touch of a man.

"Positive," he said. "Now come on...let's not drag it out."

It was the first time since he'd knocked on her door yesterday that she remembered how safe and secure she'd always felt with him. And if that had come back so quickly, she wondered how much faster everything else about the job might also fall in line.

CHAPTER NINE

Derik had meant every word he'd said just before they left the building. He had no idea how Morgan was managing to make herself face this case. She was a shell of her former self and for almost the entire short length of this renewed case, he'd sensed a haunted vibe from her. He knew he needed to talk with her at depth, to help her process what she'd been through over the past ten years.

Now that her father was gone, Derik feared he truly was all she had. Sure, there was Director Mueller, but he would always put business first. No, if Morgan was going to get out of this rut and back into some semblance of normalcy, he was going to have to be the one to push her. He knew she was more than capable of doing it herself, but he also knew she had so much more on her plate.

She was going to need a little extra push, and he was more than happy to be the one to do it, when needed.

He tried taking a baby step toward that as he drove them to the address of Engram Catholic Church, where Feeney was once again working. Ten years ago, Derik and Morgan had made something of a game of bouncing theories off of one another, briefing themselves on leads or suspects as they were in transit.

He tried it again now, noting that she'd still not bothered opening the folder.

"You just going to take my word for it that Feeney is worth looking into?" he asked.

"Yeah. Why wouldn't I?"

"No clue. Don't you at least want to know a bit about him?"

"Sure. Go ahead."

Derik recited what he'd read just before leaving, touching all the cornerstones of Feeney being a suspect, right down to the timing of it all.

"Okay," he said. "Here's what you need to know about our priest friend Andy Feeney. Like I said at the precinct, he was excommunicated from the church around the time you were arrested for the murders. And just last week, the excommunication was overturned, and he returned to his position at the same church as our fourth victim attended. He's the perfect suspect, Morgan."

"Why was he excommunicated?"

"The only thing I could find was 'differing theological opinions.' You have to keep in mind, the only reason he's in the Seven Signs Killer files at all is because of his link to the fourth victim, Sandra Berryhill. So all we have is the eerie timeline and his connection to Berryhill."

"In other words, if he has a solid alibi for the past week or so, he's not our guy."

"Right. But we have to rule him out first."

He tried to gauge her mood, trying to determine if she, too, thought Feeney was a likely suspect. But her face was a blank slate, as it had been every time he'd visited her in prison and the few occasions he'd seen her since she'd returned home. He couldn't read her anymore, and that unsettled him more than he cared to admit.

"Do me a favor," she said out of the blue.

"Maybe. What's the favor?"

"Tell me about your most exciting case while I was in prison."

He gave her a puzzled look and asked, "Are you sure? I don't want to seem like I'm bragging."

"Yes, I'm sure. I need to know everyone else's lives went on as usual while I was away."

He sighed and thought back through his past decade. There were plenty of cases to choose from, but the eight-month job regarding a hidden drug ring in the basement of a daycare was the big exclamation point. And as he told her the details, he realized he enjoyed sharing them with her. He told her every detail as if he might be telling a kid a bedtime story.

"So I was part of this massive drug bust…where we found a huge drug ring operating out of the basement of a daycare center."

"Oh my God. How did that go?"

"It was a huge mess," Derik recalled with a smile. "We had to get the kids upstairs out as quickly as possible and then we were sorting through drugs and paraphernalia for hours in their playroom. It was insane.

"We had to use undercover agents to infiltrate the operation, and we found out there were kids being used as drug mules. We had to be incredibly careful because we didn't want the kids to get hurt in the takedown."

Morgan's eyes widened, the first spark of enthusiasm Derik had seen in a while. "That's crazy. You guys were able to take everyone down without anyone getting hurt?"

"Well, there were a few close calls, but we managed to get everyone out safely. And the satisfaction of shutting down that operation. It ended up with about twenty kids needing a new daycare, of course."

Morgan smiled weakly. "That does sound exciting."

"But don't forget," Derik added, "we're working on a pretty exciting case now too. And remember, you're not alone. We're in this together."

"Yeah, I know."

Still, she thought of all the cases she'd missed with him...of the setback her career had suffered because of her absence.

She continued to dwell silently on this until they reached the church eight minutes later. Engram Catholic Church was a small, unremarkable building, made of brick and surrounded by a small patch of struggling grass. Derik looked over at Morgan, who was staring at the building with a look of intense concentration.

"You okay?" he asked.

She nodded and opened the passenger side door, anxious to get back on track. "Let's go."

Derik waited just a moment, watching her as she got out. He was beginning to understand just how big of a mistake Mueller and his little team had made by inviting her into this case so quickly after her release from prison. This was not the same Morgan Cross who had kicked so much ass ten years ago. More than that, this very different, plodding Morgan was wrestling with things none of them could possibly begin to understand.

They crossed a small sidewalk and entered the church. The doors opened up into what looked like a large foyer, adorned with an oak desk, a coat rack, and a small statue of a religious icon Derik wasn't familiar with. A set of double doors ahead of them stood open, revealing the simple yet quite beautiful nave. Peering in as they passed through the doors, Derik saw two men speaking near the front of the room, just in front of the pulpit. They were both older men, dressed in priestly garb. They noticed the agents entering the room at once.

The one closest to them, a man of about sixty or so and quite tall, took a single step toward them. "Can I help you?"

"Yes," Derik said. "We're looking for a priest by the name of Andy Feeney."

The tall man frowned slightly and looked over at the second priest. That priest, about six inches shorter than the other and maybe five or ten years younger, gave a small, guilty-looking wave. "That's me. And…well, who are you?"

Derik gave Morgan the opportunity to show her badge, but she remained quiet and unmoving. She seemed, at the moment, to be completely checked out.

Derik showed his ID. "Agents Greene and Cross. We'd like to ask you some questions."

Feeney looked absolutely aghast but began to nod. "Okay…can I ask what this is about?"

"Yes. But is there somewhere we can speak in private?"

"Yes, of course."

Feeney looked both guilty and embarrassed as he stepped away from the other priest and led them to a small room off to the side of the nave. It was a tiny office, just as nice and polished-looking as the rest of the church. The room was sparse, with just a table and a few chairs. Feeney closed the door behind them as Derik and Morgan sat down in matching chairs. Feeney remained standing.

"What can I help you with?" Feeney asked, his voice shaking slightly.

"We're investigating a series of murders that have taken place in the area," Derik said. "And we have reason to believe that you may be able to help us with our investigation."

Feeney's eyes widened. "Me? How so?"

"We understand that you were excommunicated from the church around the same time as the murders began ten years ago. And that you just recently returned to your position at this church, correct?"

"Yes…"

"Well, these murders…they started a little over ten years ago and then stopped. But then they started up several days ago…right around the same time you returned to the church. The timeline fits your excommunication journey perfectly, just as the murders started up again."

Feeney looked like he was going to faint, a look of utter confusion coming across his face. "I…I see. But I assure you, I had nothing to do with any murders."

"We're not accusing you of anything," Derik said. "We just need to rule you out as a suspect."

Feeney nodded quickly. "Yes, but…why even suspect me at all?"

"The fourth victim attended this church ten years ago," Morgan said, speaking for the first time since entering the church. "A woman named Sandra Berryhill."

Feeney's eyes widened in surprise. "Sandra...I knew her, yes. She was a parishioner here for a while. And I do remember her being murdered...it was a terrible time. But I don't know what you're getting at."

"Mr. Feeney, what did you do for the ten years you weren't with the church?"

"I...I moved out to Arizona for a bit to be with my mother in her last months. She died of cancer eight years ago. I stayed out there with family for a bit and then spent some time in London. I came back to the States about two years ago and have been living here ever since."

"And why did you return to the church?"

Feeney looked taken aback by the question, but quickly composed himself. "Well, after my mother passed, I spent my time reflecting on my faith and my beliefs. I traveled, as I said. I did some volunteer work, and I even wrote a book."

"A book?" Derik raised an eyebrow. "What kind of book?"

"It was a theological work, exploring some of the more controversial aspects of the Catholic faith."

"Mm-hmm." Derik leaned back in his chair. "And why were you excommunicated in the first place?"

Feeney shrugged as if it were no big deal. "Differences in opinions on baptism and communion methods. I know it sounds small and silly, but in the Catholic church, it's a pretty big deal. I was angry when I left...thought I'd never come back. Thought they'd never *let* me back. I had quite a few arguments on my way out, and I was very outspoken."

Derik nodded, knowing that getting these stories backed up would be very easy. Just a few conversations with other priests and clergymen within the church.

"Mr. Feeney, do you know anyone by the name of Samson? Even if it's just a nickname?"

He thought about it for a moment before shaking his head. "No, I don't believe I do."

"Can you provide alibis for your whereabouts over the past week?" Morgan asked.

Derik was glad to hear her speaking. Her voice seemed softer now, something he'd come to expect in interrogations and interviews. When they'd worked closely together in the past, this was more or less a tell for her...a sign that she was pretty sure the person they were speaking to wasn't the person they were looking for.

"Yes. I...I have a second job. I put my notice in when I knew I was coming back to the church, but I was asked to finish out the month."

49

"And where is that job?"

That embarrassed look came to his face again. "Stocking shelves at a supermarket. It's the night shift, from eleven to five. It's what I did for two years since moving back to the States."

"And you've done it every night this week?"

"Yes. And I'm here during the days. I'm only getting about four hours of sleep a day, but it's okay. I've taken a week off once the month at the supermarket is up. I'll catch up on my rest then."

Derik looked over to Morgan. She met his gaze and nodded. She stood up quickly and gave Feeney a little nod. "Please make sure you don't leave town for a while. We may need to call on you with additional questions."

"No worries there," Feeney said, relieved. "With my work schedule for the next two weeks, there's no way I could leave town at all."

Morgan left the small office without saying a word. Derik got up to go after her, giving Feeney a quick "Thank you" on his way out.

He caught up to Morgan just as she reached the sidewalk outside. He nearly held a hand out to stop her but thought better of it. She was far too unpredictable.

"Morgan. Jesus, what's going on?"

"Nothing."

"You're angry about something."

"You're right," she said. They were at the car now, and she stopped at the trunk to glare at him. "I'm mad and frustrated. I…I didn't even want to get back into this and now I feel like I'm failing all over again. I feel like I stepped right back into this case without any sort of time to myself after prison. I came right back and now…now I'm failing all over again."

"But Morgan…you can't—"

"No. You asked, and I told you. That's it. We can maybe talk it out later, but not right now. Right now, all I want to do is find this asshole. I have to close this, Derik. And I…I want to go home for a bit. Just to sit, to think."

"Yeah," he said. "Yeah, I think that's a good idea." What he thought, but didn't say, was: *Maybe that's where you should have stayed all along. It was madness to bring you back into this so soon.*

When she turned away, Derik was pretty sure he'd seen the glimmer of tears in her eyes. He stood motionless as Morgan got into the car and slammed the door. Then, after taking a slow, calming breath, Derik also got into the car. And when he started the engine and pulled back out into the road, he let Morgan have her silence.

50

As he glanced over at her, he saw that the hints of tears were gone. There was now a steely look in her eyes…another sign he had come to know well. Sometimes she'd get a look in her eyes that made it seem like she was staring way off into the distance.

She was doing it now and Derik smiled when he saw the ghost of his former partner lurking behind her eyes.

What that expression meant was that she was locked in. She was focusing hard, putting the pieces together.

It was a very small step, but he dared to think that her outbursts throughout the day had paid off. Maybe, just maybe, he was on the verge of getting his old partner back.

CHAPTER TEN

Morgan Cross was officially back and on the case. This pleased and surprised him. He figured it would take at least a few weeks for the bureau to get back into the thick of things. But they'd wasted no time and had pulled her in right away.

He wondered idly if he should be nervous about this. Had Morgan sat in prison for those ten long years, fixating only on the case...on his work? Had she been released from prison like a rodeo bull from its gate, charging toward anything that dared to flash red in front of her?

He rather hoped so. He was down to just one sign remaining. It would have to be a good one. If it was the sign he was to go out on, it really needed to be something special. And in a strange way, a small part of him almost hoped Morgan was able to catch him. She'd been so dedicated to catching him a decade ago, her every waking moment spent trying to hunt him down.

In a way, this seventh sign was as much hers as it was his. That's how he liked to see it, anyway.

It had been torture to wait for her to get out of prison. He'd more or less designed the chain of events that had put her there, but he'd never in his wildest dreams imagined that the idiot courts and judicial system would put her away for ten years.

Maybe it was because of those ten years that he was working so quickly. The drowning victims, the blind man, and now the seventh sign. His eleventh victim. He'd do it tonight, meaning he would have taken six lives in less than a week. Ten years ago, he'd staggered them out. He'd gone a full two weeks between the third and fourth signs.

On a few occasions, he'd almost started up again while Morgan had been away. But he'd fought the urge both times, feeling deep in his soul that she was to be a part of this...that she needed to be there with him at the end.

When the urges came, they were hard to battle. But when they weren't there, life had been pretty easy. He'd kept himself busy with his job and his hobbies. The job was nothing special, just running simple coding for a few backend developers for a small banking system.

His hobbies, on the other hand, had gotten quite interesting and kept his mind active. They were hobbies he never thought he'd enjoy, things he thought he might go to his grave not sharing with anyone.

He had spent six years perfecting the art of knot-tying. He found it to be very therapeutic and would get excited when there was a new one to learn. He'd followed some videos on the internet but really enjoyed checking books out from the library and following along. From modern-day, simple knots all the way back to the knots they'd used on fishing vessels during the Roman Empire, he knew them all now. He loved the way the ropes felt in his hands, how his fingers could mold and control their shapes.

He had also become deeply fascinated with the art of taxidermy. He enjoyed the way he could create something beautiful and preserve it forever. To him, it was like creating a new creature. He had a few examples in his basement at home, but only a few. After a while, the taxidermy had reminded him of what he really wanted to be doing. So he'd put a stop to it before too much interest had been expelled.

But that was then, while he'd been waiting. Now, things were moving right along. Morgan was back and his work was back on track.

He already had a victim in mind and was forcing himself to wait it out. For now, he sat a block away from the apartment building of the dead blind man. He'd watched the hectic flow of cops in and out of the building. He'd even spotted Morgan and her partner. When he spotted her, he couldn't help but feel a sense of admiration for her. She was determined, focused, and relentless in her pursuit of justice. It was these qualities that had made her his ultimate nemesis all those years ago. And now she was back and fully invested in the case. He'd always known she was a tenacious one, but to see her back in action after ten years was impressive.

He'd been very confused about how he felt upon seeing Morgan. He supposed he needed to fully understand it before he killed tonight...before he finished his work. While he knew it was impossible, he wished he could see her up close and in action before he took this eleventh life. Ten years...surely it could change someone. He couldn't help but wonder if she was the same person she had been before. Had the ten years in prison changed her? Had it dulled her senses or weakened her resolve?

Did she still understand the weight and importance of what he was doing? Did she still want to stop him as a means of justice and what she thought was right, or was it just revenge?

With a sigh, he stood up from the bench and took one last look at the apartment.

He'd know soon enough.

More than that, he'd see her up close and personal before the day was done. He felt certain of that. And he also felt certain it would mean the death of one of them.

He wasn't sure about Morgan Cross, but as for him…well, he wasn't nearly ready to die.

CHAPTER ELEVEN

Skunk greeted Morgan warmly as she walked through the front door. She made a fuss over him for a moment, petting him and calling him a good boy, before allowing him outside to do his business. As he set about this, Morgan stood in the doorway of her father's house, peering inside and wondering if it would ever truly feel like home again.

She wasn't a big believer in the supernatural, but she wondered if she might find it easier to accept the place as her own if her father haunted the place. If there were such things as ghosts, her father would certainly be the sort to take up residence in his home just to screw with people.

Maybe he *was* there. Maybe he was there and she just couldn't see him. After all, she was already being haunted by the Seven Signs Killer case. What was one more ghost in her life?

Done in the yard, Skunk came rushing back through the doorway and led her inside. He'd certainly had no problems quickly thinking of this place as his home. He sat down in the middle of the living room floor, cozy on the old rug, and looked up at her as if to ask what their plans were for the rest of the day.

She sat down on the floor with him and tried to sort it all out. While she didn't regret hopping on the Seven Signs Killer case right away, she did feel it would have been more prudent to wait a while. Now, not only did she have that case to worry about, but she had the daunting task of trying to reinsert herself into society.

She needed to sort out her current cellphone situation. The burner she'd been using was fine for now, but wouldn't be a viable solution for very long. She needed to officially switch the electric bill, water bill, and all other utilities over to her name. Small things, sure, but they needed to be done.

She sat on the rug and managed to pull memories of her father to the front of her mind, temporarily obliterating the worries and stress of the case. She remembered him clearly in that moment, focusing in on some of her favorite memories.

She remembered how her father used to take her fishing when she was a little girl. He'd pack a lunch and they'd spend the whole day out in the sun, casting their lines and chatting about life. The smell of the water and the sound of the birds chirping around them. She remembered how proud he was of her when she caught her first fish. He used to tell her that fishing was a lot like life—you never really knew what you were going to catch, but you had to be patient and willing to take risks.

Another memory came to her, of her and her father sitting on the front porch of this very house just a few months before she'd left for Quantico to start her career with the bureau. Sipping on cheap beer and watching the world go by. They'd talked about everything and nothing, just enjoying each other's company. She could feel the warmth of the sun on her skin, and the gentle breeze rustling through her hair.

She didn't realize it until prison, but those evenings of doing nothing on the porch were some of her favorite memories she had of him. Between conversations, they'd play songs from their respective childhoods. Her father had done his best to get her into Bread, Janis Joplin, and the Beach Boys. And while she did have a soft spot for Janis Joplin, she didn't think anything would ever quite top Nirvana— just a bit before her teenage years, but still her favorite. Her father, to his credit, had learned all the words to "Smells Like Teen Spirit" even though he despised the band.

Thinking of him singing that brutal chorus between sips of beer out on the porch pulled fiercely at her heart. Morgan's eyes drifted closed as she allowed herself to fully immerse in these memories, to feel them as if they were happening right now. She could hear her father's voice and smell his aftershave.

As she sat there, lost in thought, her phone rang. She jumped, startled out of her reverie, and fished it out of her pocket. It was a local number.

"Hello?" she answered.

"Is this Ms. Cross? Ms. Morgan Cross?"

"Yes. Who's speaking?"

"My name is Thomas Grace, calling from the county's Treasury office. I was hoping to speak with you about your father's home...a home I see that he left to you when he passed."

"Yeah, okay. What about it?"

"Well, there's no gentle way to put this, but there's a considerable amount of back taxes still owed on the property...an oversight by your father and his accountant, I'm sure."

"Okay. So what needs to be done?" She made sure to keep her tone harsh, wanting to make it clear that she had no time for this bullshit.

"Well, Ms. Cross, the taxes need to be paid in full as soon as possible. The deadline for payment is fast approaching, and if they aren't paid, we'll have no choice but to begin the foreclosure process."

Morgan sighed and ran a hand through her hair. "Fine. How much do I owe?"

Thomas cleared his throat. "It's quite a hefty sum, I'm afraid. A total of thirty-one thousand dollars."

"Are you serious?"

"Yes, I'm afraid I am."

She wondered, briefly, how Thomas Grace had gotten the number to her burner phone. Maybe the prison, perhaps? She didn't know. And really, it didn't matter. She was just trying to place blame somewhere, something she knew was a waste of time.

"When do you need it?" she asked, trying to make sure she kept her calm. The last thing she needed on her plate right now was an angry exchange with the county Treasury office.

"As soon as possible, Ms. Cross. We can work out a payment plan if necessary, but the sooner the better."

"You said it might be an oversight by his accountant, yes?"

"That's right," Thomas said.

"Do you have his name and number?"

"I do. One moment, please."

Thomas took a second and then gave her the name and number of her father's accountant. Morgan knew it was irresponsible and immature, but she did nothing about it. She did not write the name or the number down. Besides, she figured all of that information was in one of the shoeboxes in her dad's closet. For right now, though, she simply didn't feel like bothering with it.

"Got it?" Thomas asked.

"Got it."

"Good. Now if you have any—"

"Sounds good."

With that, she ended the call and threw the phone over onto the couch in disgust. She could feel Skunk nuzzle up to her, sensing her distress. She wrapped her arms around him tightly, wanting nothing more than to bury her face in his fur.

It was in that moment that Morgan realized that she couldn't do this alone. She needed help, and not just with the finances. She needed someone to talk to. There was Derik but she'd somehow managed to alienate herself from him for the time being. Also, they had enough to deal with in trying to find their old work groove as they attempted to stop this killer from taking his eleventh victim.

There was also sweet Lora Foster next door, but the idea of trying to talk to her about her troubles was terrifying. And a bit irritating. The woman meant well, but if Morgan remembered correctly, she spoke as if she was being charged per word.

As all of this cycled through her head, Skunk continued to snuggle in beside her as she lay back and stretched out. For now, she supposed he would do in place of an actual human. It was cozy, actually, to be lying on the rug of her father's living room with her old dog.

It was so cozy that when her phone rang again, she sat up quickly and realized she'd dozed off on the rug. Bleary-eyed and momentarily confused, she nearly decided to ignore the call. It would probably just be someone else letting her know that she was now responsible for paying for things her father had not been aware of.

But the Seven Signs Killer lurked in her mind as well. Maybe the call was about the case.

She got to her feet and walked over to the couch, where she'd thrown the phone before her unexpected nap. She was pretty sure it was Derik. She again considered not answering it for a moment but, unable to take the suspense, answered on the fourth ring.

"Hello?"

"Morgan, it's me," Derik said. "If you're up to it, we just got a call from the ME. He says he'd like to see us concerning Victor Rhyman. I have no issue going on my own, but—"

"No, I'm good. Do you want to come by the house to pick me up?"

"It just shows how well I know you," he said. "I knew you'd come along…I'm about five minutes away right now."

"I'll see you then," she said, not appreciating his little jab.

She looked at Skunk lovingly and shook her head. "What the hell is wrong with me, boy?"

He wagged his tail as if to say he didn't think there was anything at all wrong with her. That, in his eyes, she was perfectly fine. It wasn't much, but she took that bit of encouragement as she shook the vestiges of sleep away and waited for Derik to arrive.

***

The medical examiner was a fifty-eight-year-old overweight man named Smith who greeted them with a bit too much enthusiasm for a man with his career. Morgan had always appreciated the grisly work medical examiners had to do, but the ones who seemed to REALLY enjoy their job seemed slightly odd to her.

Morgan let Derik lead the conversation as they entered the examination room. She still felt slightly off, almost like a kid playing pretend in the shadow of people doing actual, dangerous work.

The body of Victor Rhyman was on the examination table, nude, his lower half covered with a sheet. The gruesome way in which he'd been stabbed in the eyes was quite terrible to look at.

"So what were you able to find so quickly?" Derik asked. "You haven't had the body that long, right?"

"Two hours, give or take," Smith said. "Anyway, as for what I found, it's a bit odd, really." He pointed to Rhyman's right collarbone. "See that?"

Both Morgan and Derik leaned in closer. Morgan did see what he was talking about but wasn't sure what it was. It looked like a very faint trace of a red powder—something that reminded her of cayenne pepper, but a little darker. There was a small, faint streak of it, and then a few powdered flakes of it to the side.

"What is it?" Derik asked.

"That is the remnants of copper," Smith said. "Copper powder, if you will. There were also traces of it in the stab wounds in his eyes, sort of soaked up into the blood. Not much, but just enough to see with the naked eye under intense light. There were very faint traces of it in his hair as well."

"Copper?" Derik asked. "Why would there be copper on a dead blind man?"

"That's the question, isn't it?" Smith said, shaking his head. "It's not something you'd normally find in someone's eyes or hair."

Morgan's mind was racing. Copper powder? What did that have to do with anything? She couldn't make sense of it. But something about it felt important. More than that, there was something slightly familiar about it...like an itch she couldn't reach.

Derik seemed to be thinking along the same lines. "We need to know as soon as possible where that copper came from."

"Was it on the previous four victims?" Morgan asked.

"None that I found," Smith said. "Then again, they'd been drowned and if there were any traces of this dust on them, it likely got washed right off."

"Copper..." Derik said. "Jesus, that could be anything, right? It's all over the place. Wiring, construction...I don't know if this really even helps."

But then, just as he said this, Morgan was able to reach that mental itch. And it was all because of the memories of her father she'd been lost in before falling asleep on the living room floor. At first, her hunch felt like a stretch but as it settled into her stream of logic, she thought it might make all the sense in the world.

She looked at Smith and said, "You're sure it's copper?"

"Yes. I ran the test myself."

Already heading for the door, Morgan said, "Come on, Derik. I think I know where to look."

And then, without making sure he was following, Morgan left the examination room feeling somewhat upbeat for the first time since being released from prison.

CHAPTER TWELVE

Morgan was pretty sure it wasn't technically legal for her to drive. She wasn't quite sure what the rules were for someone who had just been released from prison after a decade. Her license had expired for sure. But that was the least of her worries as she drove the bureau sedan off of the four-lane and onto a two-lane road that led them into a more rural area.

"I'm uneasy enough about you driving," Derik said. "I'm also uneasy that you haven't spoken since we left the ME's office, but you seem to have a GPS system locked in your head. Want to tell me where we're going?"

They were close enough now where she didn't think she'd be able to convince herself she was wrong. Besides, now that the place she'd been thinking about was less than ten miles away, she somehow felt certain it was exactly where they needed to go.

"Earlier, when I was at the house, I was thinking about some of my fonder memories of my father," she said. "I thought about some of the fishing trips he took me on as a little girl. It was usually to the lake, but every now and then we'd go up the Eastern Ridge River. You know it?"

"I know of it, yes. But you know I'm not much of an outdoorsman. So, please…fill me in a bit more."

"There are two different places along the Eastern Ridge River that have old, retired train bridges that go across it. Located directly between them is an old mining site. I know this because my dad used to tell me stories about his grandfather working in those mines."

"Are you about to tell me those mines contained large deposits of copper?"

"That's exactly what I'm saying. I think we need to check out that old mining site."

"Seems sort of random and, dare I say, dangerous. How sure are you about this?'

She'd hoped it wouldn't come to this, to Derik asking for a proper explanation. Just like the memory of learning to drive a stick shift with her father, the little bit she knew about the mines came from conversations she'd had with him while fishing.

And again, a memory of her father came speeding at her. They'd been putting the boat on the river, having just loaded up on bait and sodas at the small store her father had frequented.

She remembered the boat straightening out and the mines coming into view on her right.

"What's that?" she'd asked, pointing to the decommissioned mine entrance.

"That's how folks used to get into the mines," her father had answered.

"Mines?"

"Yeah. Some big company used to mine copper there. My granddad worked there for a while before it closed down in the sixties."

"Copper?" she'd repeated. "Like the metal?"

"Yup. And it was just one of the many metals they'd find there. But copper was the big one. People used to come from all over to work in those mines. But they shut them down when people stopped mining...those mines are just big old tunnels in the earth. Sometimes people go in for a bit of fun and exploring and get hurt or even go missing. It's very dangerous in there."

Her father's voice faded as Morgan came back to the here and now.

"I'm pretty sure," she said, finally answering Derik.

Derik looked skeptical but also intrigued. "It's a long shot, but it's worth a try."

"It may not be as long of a shot as you're thinking. Another thing about copper, unless I'm sorely mistaken, is that it's widely used in occult practices, too. Things like redirecting energy, healing, other things I know next to nothing about. And I don't know about you, but a man who's killing based on the Seven Signs..."

"Yeah, that does seem to sort of fall in line."

They drove in excited silence for a few more minutes. Finally, Morgan slowed, looking for the old road she and her father had traveled down countless times. She took the turn and within minutes, it all started to look familiar as the river presented itself on their left, peeking through the trees. The river was calm but murky, and the trees that lined the bank were dense and overgrown.

As they pulled up to the first train bridge, Morgan's heart was pounding in her chest. She got out of the car and looked around, taking in the sight of the old, rusty metal and the churning river below.

"I take it we're walking?" Derik asked as he also stepped out.

"Yeah. But it's not far. Maybe half a mile. I have no idea what sort of condition the mining site is in, though."

With the car parked at the end of the gravel road that dead-ended at the old railroad bridge, Morgan started walking to the west. There was a thin footpath that led through knee-high grass and, after about twenty yards, a group of birches and elms. The path led down along the banks of the river and then meandered back up.

She took a moment to appreciate the scenery as they made their way down. When was the last time she'd actually walked in nature? Even something as simple as the smell of the grass had her senses in overload. As she took this in, more sounds that she may have overlooked ten years ago filtered in: the sound of the flowing river, birds calling out to one another nearby, even the buzzing of the annoying gnats that had started to circle her head.

"You're still sure about this?" Derik asked.

"I am." Not only was she sure they needed to check the mines, but she felt excitement and a sense of direction she hadn't felt in over ten years. It was impossible to look beyond it. A bomb could have gone off behind them and she would not have been distracted from her walk to the mines.

They arrived at the site of the old mine ten minutes later. Morgan had started to sweat a bit, swatting at the gnats swirling above her head. She saw that Derik was also sweating slightly, but he looked quite curious about what came next.

The mine showed signs of neglect and age. It consisted of a flat expanse of rock face that sat about two hundred feet off the river. Weeds had sprung up around what had once served as the entrance. The entrance itself was boarded up and blocked off by concrete and iron rails. Still, there were two distinct spaces along the sides where it was clear that people had come in and out of the mines in the years since its closure.

"Okay...now what?" Derik asked.

"Now," Morgan said, stepping toward the blockade, "we go in."

Without waiting for a reply from Derik, she approached the mine entrance and started to climb over the blockade. It was a challenge, but she managed to slip through a gap between the old concrete and wood where it had worn away, certainly the same passage countless local teens and intrepid, immature explorers had used in the past. Derik followed her lead, and they both made their way into the mines.

The air inside was stale and musty, and the ground beneath their feet was uneven and rocky. It was dark, too, but Derik had brought a flashlight from the car. He shone it ahead of them as they walked.

They made their way through the winding tunnels, their footsteps echoing off the walls. Morgan couldn't help the nagging feeling that they were being watched. As they walked deeper into the mine, Morgan could feel a sense of unease creeping up on her. It was as if the walls were closing in on her, suffocating her with their darkness. She tried to shake it off, focusing on the mission at hand.

She was surprised that there weren't many passages that broke off from the primary one. She spotted two but they had been blocked off much more efficiently than the major entrance out by the river. For just a moment, she felt incredibly trapped—as if there would never be a way out of here. She recalled her father telling her how dangerous this place was, how so many people had gone missing in these tunnels.

A slow, calming breath was all it took to get her back under control.

As they walked deeper into the mine, guided by the flashlight beam, Morgan started to notice the detritus of recent visitors. There were old soda cans and bottles, beer cans, even fast-food wrappers.

Morgan's heart started to race. She knew they were on the right track. She continued to follow the tunnels until she saw what looked like the end of the tunnel. They quickened their pace until they couldn't go straight anymore. Here, small pathways bent to the right and left away from the tunnel they'd been following.

"See this?" Derik asked, coming to a stop and pointing the flashlight beam down to the ground.

She looked down and saw a dusting of copper by her feet. There was much more of it here than at the beginning. She was quite sure there was copper in the walls, giving off a rather dull gleam in the glow of Derik's flashlight.

With this new discovery, they opted to take the pathway to the right and found that it was the right decision almost instantly. They both stopped for a moment, looking into the chamber ahead of them. Derik uttered a curse under his breath.

The chamber was about the size of a small bedroom, but the ceiling was at least twenty feet over their head. There were three small wooden benches in the chamber, one of which was adorned with a variety of candles. Most were white, but two were red. They were all in various stages of having been burned, the wax having pooled on the benches and the stone floor.

In the center of the floor, a perfect circle had been drawn in what looked like white chalk. There was nothing within the circle upon first inspection. But a closer look revealed smudges of more chalk and the now-familiar powder they knew as copper.

She turned her head to speak to Derik but saw that he had gone completely still, his head cocked slightly in the other direction.

"Derik? What is it?"

He held up a finger and whispered, "Wait. I thought I heard something."

Morgan's heart started pounding wildly as she looked around the chamber, her eyes darting from one corner to another. She couldn't see or hear anything other than the sound of her own breathing.

"Are you sure?" she whispered.

Derik nodded, his eyes scanning the darkness. "I thought I heard footsteps. But maybe it's just the tunnels, playing tricks on—"

He stopped, and Morgan understood why. She'd heard it this time. Definite footsteps, somewhere back out in the tunnel. When Derik moved toward the sound, leaving the chamber, Morgan followed. It was a bit embarrassing, but she did not relish the idea of being left alone in that chamber without their only source of light.

So she followed after him, but the pursuit lasted a very short time. She'd taken only two steps toward the chamber's exit when Derik suddenly let out a grunt. Morgan jumped backward in surprise and watched as he stumbled back, his flashlight beam flickering erratically.

He caught himself on the wall, the flashlight clattering to the ground. The footsteps retreated, heading deeper into the tunnel. Morgan looked down to the floor and saw that not only had Derik been hit, but he was struggling to remain conscious.

But the footfalls of the attacker were fading, getting further away. Hating to have to make such a decision, Morgan looked down at Derik. He nodded weakly at her, as if he perfectly understood the decision she'd made.

"I'll be right back," she said.

Then, leaving the flashlight with him, Morgan took off into the dark, unfamiliar tunnel ahead of her.

CHAPTER THIRTEEN

She understood right away that leaving the flashlight behind had been a mistake. Within just several steps, she was pitched into pure darkness. Her eyes had adjusted somewhat, but she was wholly unfamiliar with the tunnels...and she had to assume that the man she was chasing knew them well.

She thought of the candles in the chamber, and the sick-sounding thump she'd heard just before Derik had gone down. She was all but certain it was their killer, and as she ran after him in the darkness, she wondered how often he'd come down here. Had he been using these mines as a lair ten years ago when she'd been after him?

She kept her left arm outstretched, her hand skimming the surface of the wall as she ran. When she felt it shift to the right, she adjusted her position so she wouldn't careen off of the wall.

She could sense the killer moving in the darkness ahead, the air in front of her disturbed by his passage. And then, as if the world had shifted under her feet, she realized that that killer had turned right. This was odd, as she didn't remember seeing an off-shooting passage on the way through. But that's exactly what she thought had happened. She could sense the motion of his movement in the musty air. She reached out with her right hand, stepping a few feet in that direction. Sure enough, there was an opening there. Somehow, probably because of the direction the flashlight was shining, she and Derik had missed it on their way in.

She took the right, a small voice telling her it was a mistake, and went running deeper down into the darkness.

The killer was quick, and Morgan had to sprint at full speed to keep up with him. Her heart was pounding, the sound of her own breaths echoing in her ears. She was so focused on following the man that she didn't notice the uneven terrain beneath her feet. She tripped over a rock and fell hard on the ground.

Pain shot through her left shoulder and she gasped, struggling to get back up. She could hear the killer's footsteps getting further away, and she knew she had to act fast. With a shout of determination, she pushed herself up and started running again.

Her shoulder throbbed with every movement, but she pushed the pain aside and focused on the task at hand. The sound of her footsteps followed her, echoing off the walls. She felt as if she was running down a never-ending maze. The only thing keeping her going was the thought of catching the killer. She thought of all the people he had killed, all the families he had destroyed. He had to be stopped. He was so close, in the darkness ahead of her, and she may never get another chance.

But then she came to an intersection within the cave. She sensed it rather than saw it, though her eyes had basically adjusted and could pick up the different shades and contours along the wall. She stopped, looking to her right where another tunnel veered off at a harsh angle. The passage she was currently in bent to the left in a lazy sort of curb.

She did her best to steady her breath, trying to listen to the passages. She could hear the killer's footsteps sure enough, but it was impossible to tell which way he'd gone. The sounds down here in the darkness were hard to follow, hard to—

"Morgan!"

It was Derik's voice, coming from behind her. He sounded worried, not just in pain. In that moment, Morgan realized that she had to make a decision: she could continue venturing down tunnels she wasn't familiar with, or she could go back to make sure Derik was okay.

And for a terrifying moment, the decision was much harder than it should have been.

Morgan's gut told her to go back to Derik. She had never been one to leave anyone behind, especially not someone she cared about. But the thought of the killer getting away again made her hesitate. In the end, her loyalty to Derik won out.

She took a deep breath and turned back toward the direction of Derik's voice. She ran as fast as she could, trying to ignore the pain in her shoulder. The sound of Derik's voice grew louder as he continued to call out for her. Her heart burned with the decision of letting the killer go but as she approached the area of the original tunnel where she'd left Derik, it subsided a bit. When she arrived, she saw that he was sitting up against the wall, holding his head in his hands. The flashlight was trapped in the fork of his legs, pointing up and slightly back toward the entrance.

"What is it?" she asked. "Are you okay?"

"Woozy. Dizzy. Jesus, my head hurts. He…he hit me, didn't he?"

She then understood that he'd called out for her with such urgency because he was confused. The whack to the head had him disoriented.

"Yeah, he got you." She saw the blood coming from his hairline, a nasty cut starting the flow. "Got you good from the looks of it."

"Did you catch him?"

Morgan shook her head, feeling a pang of guilt. "No, I lost him. But you're hurt, we need to get you out of here."

Derik nodded, wincing as he tried to stand up. "I think I'll be okay."

"There's a gash on your head that says otherwise." Already, though, she was thinking of what to do next. Even if there were alternate entrances and exits to these old mines, someone must know where they were. A call to the bureau or local PD would probably reveal those answers. Maybe there was still a chance they could nab the bastard on his way out.

Morgan helped Derik to his feet, keeping a reassuring hand on his back as they made their way back out through the tunnel. The darkness seemed even more oppressive now that they didn't have the adrenaline of the chase fueling them. She held the flashlight with the hand that wasn't helping to keep Derik steady. Thankfully, it was the hand of her right arm, which she'd banged up in the tunnel. If she'd had to keep Derik up with that one, they'd both be screwed.

After what seemed like forever, they came to a little blanket of sunlight on the floor. And then, about two minutes later, they stepped out of the mine's entrance.

"I think I'm good now," Derik said. "Feeling sleepy, though. I bet it's a damned concussion."

"And at least a dozen stitches," she said, already taking her phone from her pocket. When she realized she didn't have any contacts saved in it, she shoved it back in.

"Can I use your phone?" she asked.

He nodded as they slowly made their way back along the trail that would lead them to the side of the old railroad bridge. But as he reached into his pocket for it, Derik swayed on his feet and fell. Morgan reached out for him, but missed, her busted shoulder screaming in pain. He went down in a cluster of weeds, his eyes fluttering closed.

She took his phone right away. Instead of calling the police for information on the mines, she once again put Derik's best interest at heart. She called 911, waited for the connection, and reported a potentially seriously injured FBI agent.

CHAPTER FOURTEEN

That was close.

How had he been so foolish? He'd been so careful to cover his tracks, to make sure he left no traces. Well, only the traces he wanted. They had to know who he was somehow, after all.

But he'd never expected them to learn about the mines. As he ran through the field, directly toward a stretch of forest that stretched on for several miles, he could only assume it was Morgan. He'd been oddly thrilled as the duration of her incarceration had come to its close. He wanted her out. He wanted a formidable agent coming after him. It's what kept him on his toes. It's what made the entire thing exciting to him.

He supposed waiting for her to come out of prison had been a foolish idea. Maybe almost poetic or romantic. It had felt right at the time, but now he wasn't so sure.

After all, ten years was a very long time. He wasn't as strong as he used to be, not quite as fast and reliable. His mind still felt just as sharp but at the end of the day, he wasn't sure that mattered. What he hadn't expected was Morgan's determination.

He'd been so caught up in his own plans and schemes that he'd somehow failed to understand that Morgan had likely spent the last ten years thinking about him...about the Seven Signs Killer. She'd likely been fuming and focusing on how to find and stop him when she got out.

Ten years of planning and obsessing.

Maybe he'd made a grave error.

But even if that was the case, it didn't matter. He had one more victim. One more death before the work was done. After that...well, after that, he had no idea what he would do. He'd come to enjoy killing. He wasn't so sure he could just give it up at the drop of a dime.

He was so caught up in his thoughts that he didn't even realize he'd already come to the edge of the forest. He hurried in and squatted down behind the base of a large oak. From where the strip of forest was positioned, he could see across the field he'd just come through. He'd come out of a small tunnel that was really little more than a hole in the ground...an exit Morgan and her partner would not have been able to find without an intimate knowledge of the cave system. They hadn't spent the last decade in those twisting, turning tunnels.

Across the field, the land took a slight downward tilt. Because of this, he could just barely see the shapes of Morgan and her partner coming back out of the cave. So he hadn't killed the man after all. He didn't think he had; he hadn't put a lot of power behind the blow after picking up the first sizable rock he could find.

Still, he supposed they'd have a renewed passion now, more desperate than ever to find him.

In other words, he was going to have to get moving. He'd planned on waiting until tonight to strike his eleventh victim, but he was going to have to escalate things.

He took one last look at Agent Cross and her partner. It looked as if he'd fallen down. She was hunched over him, making a call. They were so far away that he could hear nothing. He assumed she was calling for help.

He turned and started to race back through the forest, ready to get started on wrapping up his work...on getting to the next victim.

As he ran deeper into the forest, he could feel his heart pounding in his chest. It wasn't just the adrenaline from the near-miss encounter with Morgan and her partner. It was also the thrill of the hunt, the excitement of knowing he was so close to achieving his goal.

He knew exactly who his final victim was going to be. It was someone who had never crossed his path before, but someone who would be perfect for his grand finale. Like the others, he'd been following them and observing them for months. He knew their schedules and routines, right down to the code for the electronic lock on their front door.

Samson smiled as he thought about approaching that door...of the time and effort he'd put into his work. When he was done, he thought many might see his Seven Signs murders as a masterpiece. It was going to be so glorious that he thought Agent Morgan Cross might even appreciate it when all was said and done.

CHAPTER FIFTEEN

Morgan knew it was morbid, but she'd always liked hospitals. She didn't enjoy being a patient, but the act of visiting them had always filled her with a sense of peace. Even right down to the antiseptic smells of the cleaning solutions in the hallways, the slight sting of bleach, the ghost scent of the cafeteria food.

She had no idea what caused this. She'd watched her mother slowly die at a young age and had come to the hospital at least twenty times while her mother had battled cancer. Maybe, she assumed, there was some weird nostalgia and comfort there buried in her subconscious.

Whatever the case, she found it hard to sit still as she waited for an update on Derik. The initial report from the doctors when they'd arrived at the emergency room was that he would be fine. At worst, there would be some stitches involved and he almost certainly had a concussion. He'd still been very much dazed and out of sorts when they'd arrived at the hospital.

It had been forty-five minutes, and she was tired of waiting. Not just for an update on Derik, but also waiting to get out of here. Forty-five minutes gave their killer a large head start. And if he was panicking at having run into them in the caves, there was no telling how he might react now.

So she started down the hallway, heading for the little examination room they'd placed Derik in. She passed by a few visitors and nurses, one of whom was pushing along a small laptop on a stand. She felt those old memories of coming to the hospital to see her mother trying to surface, but she pushed them away as she came to the examination room. Derik was lying on the hospital bed, his head wrapped in a bandage. He looked up as she entered, a small smile forming on his lips.

"Hey, you," he said softly.

Morgan walked over to him and took his hand. "Hey, yourself. The half-wrapped head is a nice look for you."

"Oh, I know."

"Are you feeling any better?"

"Still a bit dizzy but my thoughts seem to be tracking. I think I'm okay for now."

"The last I heard, they were just talking about a few stitches. What's with the wrap?"

"Compression. There's some swelling…some very nasty swelling."

"How many stitches?"

"Twenty-two. My head still feels tingly and numb." He looked at her with a peculiar glance and said, "Did you ever get stitches?"

"When I was thirteen. I fell off a skateboard and butchered my forearm."

"But ever for work?"

"Nope. Safety first when on the job," she said with a chuckle.

"Laugh all you want," Derik said. "But you know…you did save my life back there. That was some very quick thinking. And I know it had to be hard for you to let Samson go to come back and get me."

"Maybe it was," she said with a smile. "But I think I made the right choice. Besides…you know, you saved my life, too."

"How do you figure that?"

She knew what she wanted to say, but it was harder to get out than she'd expected. She took a deep breath and tried her best. "When I was in prison, I always knew I had at least one person who knew I was innocent…someone who knew from the very first moment the ridiculous case started that I was innocent. Some days that was all I had to hang on to. So…I really appreciate that."

He looked away from her. She supposed it was to not let her see his reaction. Looking at the ceiling, though, he did his best to reply.

"Morgan, you don't have to thank me. That's what partners do, right? We have each other's backs."

Morgan nodded, accepting his words even though they didn't fully capture the depth of her gratitude. "Yeah, you're right. We do have each other's backs."

"And another thing…you're a good friend, Morgan. Always have been. I know I haven't always shown it, but I do appreciate you. And it wasn't hard to know you were innocent. You're too good of a person to ever do something like that. You can be a bit of a pain in the ass at times, but you have a good heart."

She smiled, feeling a weight lift from her shoulders. "Thank you, Derik. That means a lot."

There was a moment of silence between them before Derik spoke again. "How are you feeling about Samson getting away?"

Morgan's expression darkened at the mention of the killer's name. "Pissed, honestly. I can't believe we let him slip through our fingers like that."

"We don't know for sure it was him," Derik pointed out.

She knew this was true but for some reason, hearing it spoken out loud stung. When she'd been down there in the dark, she'd wanted it to be him so badly that nothing else made sense. But now, out of the mines and with Derik being injured, it was easier to see other possibilities.

"Speaking of which," Morgan said, turning back for the door, "I should probably check in with Mueller and let him know how you are. I'm sure he'll be irate that we were that close only to come out empty-handed. But I'll be back soon, okay?"

"Um, no. You can't let Mueller know you were with me. You were supposed to be home, remember?"

"I do. But...I think this can help us both. I'll say I called you and said I had a lead but wouldn't share it unless you let me tag along."

"He knows you don't have that sort of sway over me."

Morgan smirked. "Oh, we'll see. Besides...in the event this guy *was* our killer, those mines need to be thoroughly searched."

"If you call Mueller right now, you're going to be getting yourself into more trouble."

"I know," she said. And then, with a smile, she added: "But what's he going to do? Fire me?"

"Morgan..."

"It'll be okay, Derik. Remember how you used to trust me?"

"Yes...and I still do."

Derik gave her a wave of dismissal before closing his eyes to rest. Morgan walked out of the examination room, heading back down the hallway toward the waiting room. She passed by a group of nurses gossiping about some doctor's personal life, and she tried not to eavesdrop.

Besides, she barely heard it at all. She was too busy appreciating what had just happened in Derik's room. It was the first time since he'd showed up at her house upon her release that she'd felt some of the old chemistry between them—not a romantic sort of chemistry, but a bond that existed only between agents who respected and trusted one another.

Even their playful bickering seemed to have found its footing. And in realizing all of this, Morgan understood just how badly she'd missed Derik while in prison. She had indeed held on to his belief in her innocence, but now that she was out and could see him face to face, it was an entirely different sort of exchange.

73

Not sure how the conversation with Mueller was going to go, she took the elevator down to the lobby and stepped out onto the sidewalk. She took a seat on a little bench near some flowers on the western side of the property and made the call.

She'd called once the ambulance had picked Derik up and left a vague message with Mueller's assistant asking him to call her. He hadn't called back yet.

Since it was clear Derik was going to be okay, Morgan doubted the conversation would be as quick and polite. She'd nearly forgotten about Mueller's temper. He was usually kind and level-headed but he had never been able to receive bad news without losing his cool.

She placed the call, perfectly ready to trade barbs with him if it came down to it. After all, the way she saw it, she was doing them a favor by even being on this damned case so soon after her release from prison.

The phone rang in her ear twice before Mueller picked up. There was no hello or pleasantries. He got straight to the point, which Morgan actually appreciated.

"Agent Cross, what is it?" Mueller's voice was brusque.

"I thought you should know that Derik is in the hospital. He got whacked on the head, but he's going to be okay. A few stitches and some swelling, likely a concussion."

"What? What the hell happened?"

She told him, starting with the lie she and Derik had discussed— about how she'd bullied him into allowing her to come along. Everything from that point on, she kept truthful.

When she was done, she could practically feel the fury coming from Mueller's end of the phone. "I don't know which of you to be madder at."

"I'll take it. But this is sort of on you...just like you said when we brought in Black. You should have known not to dangle this carrot in front of me. To expect me not to bite...what were you thinking?"

"Watch your tone, Cross."

She let out a deep breath, not sure how she felt about the indifference coursing through her. She really didn't give a damn what Mueller was thinking at this point.

"Derik is stable and resting now," she said. "Twenty or so stitches and a swollen head. Most likely a concussion as well. But I just spoke to him, and he seems coherent."

There was a brief moment of silence on the other end of the line before Mueller spoke again, his tone slightly softer. Perhaps he had decided to roll with the punches, to see what might come of this. "I see. That's good news, at least. And what about Samson?"

"No idea. And honestly, there's no way to know for certain it was him, but I have a feeling that—"

"So Agent Greene was attacked because of a feeling you had?"

She ignored this jab and said, "But if you can send a team down there and check the place over, I think—"

"Absolutely not. I know you think you have the best interests of everyone at heart, Agent Cross, but I'm not sending a team of agents into an abandoned mine on a hunch. At most, the way I see it, we have a vagrant on the loose that was living down in those mines and attacked when someone surprised him."

"Where's your proof?" Morgan asked.

"Where's *yours*?" Mueller roared into the phone. He cleared his throat and Morgan was certain that when he spoke again, it would be to end this entire thing. Instead, he surprised her when he asked: "Let's say this *was* Samson. You said you chased him for a good amount of time. Do you have any idea where he might have been headed?"

"No, sir. He was somewhere further back in the caves. He moved through them like he knew them well. There was no way I—"

"Agent Cross, I have another call on the line. Hold one second."

While she was placed on hold, she breathed a sigh of relief. His reaction hadn't been nearly as bad as she'd expected. Not that she cared, really. Yes, she had always thought she'd eventually want her job back, but not to the point of cowering at Mueller's occasional rants. She again reminded herself that she was doing them a favor here. The way she saw it, she had them under her thumb.

Mueller came back on the line. His voice was fast and irritated, as if the twenty-second conversation he'd just had had upset him greatly.

"Agent Cross...a body was just found...over on Dutton Road. It's very fresh and we're almost certain it's Samson's seventh sign."

"You...what?"

Shock reached through her and grabbed her heart. She suddenly found it very hard to breathe, let alone move.

"Samson's seventh sign...and eleventh victim overall. There was a note. Brief and to the point. It was—"

"Who's there now?"

"Two officers with the local PD."

"Send me the address."

"No."

75

"Fine. Then send Whitmore or someone else who doesn't have nearly as much experience with Samson as I do. And then worry and worry and fret and end up calling me in about six or seven hours anyway. I'm just trying to save you some time."

There was a pause on the other end, as Mueller was clearly not accustomed to taking orders like this from agents. But in the end, he didn't argue.

"I'll text it the moment we get off the phone. But Cross…if this is indeed the seventh sign and he's considering this thing done…"

Morgan didn't even think twice about ending the call. She didn't want to hear his theories or assumptions about how Samson might go into hiding now that it was done. No…he'd waited for her to come out of prison before he finished his work. For some reason, he saw them as connected…that he could not finish his work without her in pursuit of him.

And if the bastard truly wanted to be chased even now that his work was done, she was more than happy to oblige.

CHAPTER SIXTEEN

"Subtle," Morgan said as she sped the car down Dutton Road.

It was a road just on the outskirts of the city, an avenue that led onto two of the city's main thoroughfares from both the southern and northern routes. There was very little on the road, so as she turned onto it, Samson's intent became clear.

The second building on Dutton Road was quite large and stuck out easily. It was Seabry Funeral Home, a long one-story building that looked like most funeral homes—both serene and kind of creepy at the same time. She took the place in as she passed by, unable to shake the almost iconic significance of it as she traveled to the site of the eleventh murder.

It was less than half a mile away, a bit further down Dutton Road. The two-story home sat a good distance off the road, separated from the road by a lush, well-maintained yard. It was the home of Leonard Seabry, owner and director of Seabry Funeral Home.

He was apparently the victim that signified the seventh sign. Though Morgan wasn't religious, she'd studied this case so much that she could recite the passages of scripture that covered the seven signs. The seventh sign was the raising of Lazarus, where Jesus had resurrected a dead man.

The connection was almost cheesy…killing a funeral home director in an attempt to correlate with the raising of the dead. It made her wonder if this had been Samson's plan all along or if he was in a hurry now because of this morning and had struck at the first thing he thought seemed like it might fit the theological echoes of the seventh sign.

She pulled into the paved driveway and parked behind one of the two police cars that were already there. She made her way to the front porch, feeling a bit of new worry creep in. What if the killer did indeed disappear after this eleventh murder? How much harder would it be to find the bastard? And would he stop there or find some other reason to kill?

She had no idea. All she knew was that there was a dead man just beyond the front door and his body may be able to lead her to Samson. With her heart tightening in her chest, Morgan opened the door and stepped inside where three police officers were already on the scene.

The living room was spacious, with vaulted ceilings that gave the room an airy feel despite the weight of the situation. But the joy of the space was quickly overshadowed by the presence of the dead body. Morgan's eyes quickly scanned the room, taking everything in—the positioning of the body, the surrounding furniture, the doorways, the windows, the three cops.

As she made her way toward the body, the metallic scent of blood filled her nostrils. Leonard Seabry lay on the floor, his eyes still open in a frozen gaze. His throat had been slashed and his eyes stared blankly at the ceiling. Blood pooled around the wound on his chest where the killer had struck.

Morgan felt a deep anger bubble up inside of her. This was the eleventh victim, and yet they still had no real leads or suspects. She knelt down beside the body, carefully studying the wound. It looked like it had been made with a sharp, pointed object. It had been hurried and violent. There was no set-up or dramatic effect like with the others.

Yeah, Morgan thought. He's scared now. He was in a hurry to get this done. He knows I'm close.

"Have you checked the place over yet?" Morgan asked the cops without looking back at them.

"Yeah," one of the officers said. "Everything looked normal until we got to his office."

"Are forensics and the coroner on the way?"

"Yeah."

The man sounded almost annoyed that she was there. She knew she had a bit of a reputation, even outside of having spent a decade in jail. Morgan couldn't help but wonder if this officer speaking to her knew that she'd just gotten out. And if so, maybe he held a negative opinion of her. Maybe he was among those who assumed she'd been guilty of murder from the very start.

She really didn't care. She stood up, moved away from the body, and made her way out of the living room. She didn't want to give the cop the satisfaction of asking him where the office was, so she explored the house on her own as she looked for it.

Eventually, she found her way to the office, a smaller room off of the main hall near the stairs. There was a desk and some filing cabinets against one wall, and the walls were lined with framed awards and photographs of the funeral home. The room itself was clean and mostly organized, but it lacked life. It was clear that Seabry hadn't spent much time in this room.

But as soon as she stepped inside, she saw the oddity that the officers had mentioned. There were several pieces of paper stuck to the ceiling. Morgan looked up, doing her best to make sense of it. When she tilted her head up, a little flare of pain shot through the shoulder she'd hurt in the mine just two and a half hours ago.

Because she had to look at the papers upside down, it took her a moment to understand what she was seeing. Finally, though, she understood. And it chilled her.

The papers were folded…cheap printouts that would be handed out at a funeral. They were programs or whatever the handouts at funerals were properly called. There were eighteen of them taped up there. The faces of the dead looked down on her, most in color but some in black and white.

The raising of the dead, she thought. *Clever.*

Oh, but it pissed her off, too. He'd gone through with the murder very quickly but had taken the time to do this…to really rub her nose in it.

Angry, she stormed over to the filing cabinets. As she reached for the handle to the top drawer, she nearly stopped herself. She could very well be contaminating evidence. The killer's prints could be on the handles.

But in that moment, she was just too angry to care. Maybe if hadn't spent ten years away from the job, her instincts and dedication to the process would have served her better, she supposed.

Morgan pulled open the top drawer of the filing cabinet and began to rummage around the contents. It was filled with documents relating to the funeral home and its business. Apparently, Seabry had been quite successful. Morgan then tried the second drawer, browsing the documents for a few minutes before she came across a thick folder. She looked inside and saw printouts just like the ones on the ceiling. Leonard Seabry had apparently kept a copy of every program from each service his funeral home held.

And the killer had gone through them, taping some up on the ceiling.

"Tape," she said.

She closed the drawers and looked back up at the printouts. From what she could see, it was clear, one-sided scotch tape. They'd pick up fingerprints flawlessly. Of course, if he'd been wearing gloves, it wouldn't matter.

There was a knock at the door. She looked to the doorway and saw one of the officers standing there. "Agent Cross? I thought you'd want to know that the doorbell company just called with the log-in information to get to the security footage."

"What?"

"The doorbell…it's equipped with a camera. We can get to the footage now."

"Oh, thanks." Her brain seemed to be working overtime. Sure, it had only been ten years, but ten years ago, it wasn't all that common for people to have electronic doorbells with built-in security cameras.

With one last look up at the printouts, Morgan headed back out into the hallway. She realized that she was hesitant to revisit the body because she felt it was solely her fault. Maybe if she'd just gone after Samson for a while longer in the mines, she would have found him. Maybe she would have stopped him. After all, as it turned out, Derik's injury wasn't all that serious.

But there's no way you could have known that, she told herself. She was trying to summon up the humility to ask how she might start looking at the security footage when her phone rang. She took it out at once, hoping it might be Derik calling to let her know the hospital was releasing him.

"This is Cross," she answered.

"Cross, it's Mueller. Where are you?"

"I'm at the address you gave me. Leonard Seabry is very much dead. And there's no doubt that this was the eleventh victim…part of Samson's quest. There are—"

"Cross, I'm going to relieve you."

She heard him and she knew what he meant, but she still couldn't stop herself from saying: "What?"

"I'm taking you off this case. And while I'd love to lay all the blame at your feet, I think it comes down to our team here. We were desperate, and we thought you were the best bet at stopping this guy. But I don't think you're ready. And damn it, I should have known that from the start."

"Yeah, you should have known that. You're right. But right now, I'm standing in the living room of a man who has been dead for less than two hours. I've got a killer rubbing my face in it. And he's also in a hurry and scared because I nearly nabbed him this morning. It's the closest I've ever been, even from ten years back when I was originally after him. If you take me off of this now—"

"There's no if, Cross. I'm taking you off. Now, we can talk about you coming back in on a full-time basis in a few weeks. You have to get acclimated to normal life first."

"You're serious about this?"

"I am."

The rage that built up in her was unlike any she'd ever felt before. She felt used and unwanted. She felt as if she'd been manipulated. There was so much she wanted to say. But none of it would be productive. It would only make things worse.

"Cross? Are you there?"

Instead of responding, Morgan let some of the anger out. She raised her hand over her head and slammed the phone down onto Leonard Seabry's hardwood floor. It shattered upon impact, and Morgan was making her way to the front door before all of the little pieces were done skittering and clattering along the hardwood.

With her heart slamming and the rage still pushing her forward, Morgan knew she couldn't stop. She'd risk being arrested or even killed if that's what it took to bring this bastard in. One thing she did know, though, was that she needed to get away from the Seabry residence as fast as possible. Mueller knew that's where she was so the farther away she could get right away, the better.

She got back into the bureau sedan and instantly cranked it, shifting into reverse. She figured she'd go back to the hospital and tell Derik what had happened. Whether or not she would tell him that she intended to keep looking for Samson despite being yanked from the case, she wasn't sure.

She thought once more about how badly she wanted to find Samson, to either bring him in or even kill him. It was her driving force right now. Hell, it had been one of the only things that kept her going while in prison. She'd opened up to a few women about it, inmates who seemed to have a level head on their shoulders.

Kimmy Byers had told her that Samson, the Seven Signs Killer, had become her little god. The thing she looked to in order to feel alive. Kimmy had said lots of people had little gods that were bad gods...people wanting to get out only to go back to an old addiction, or to a toxic spouse.

But Kimmy had been a little wacky. She'd been...

Morgan's sudden realization was so shocking and sudden that she nearly ran through the red light at the intersection near the northern end of Dutton Road. She hit the brakes, thinking of Kimmy Byers, and wondering if the answer had been staring her right in the face all along.

CHAPTER SEVENTEEN

Morgan thought of Kimmy Byers as she hurried back to the hospital. Kimmy had been quiet and reserved during her first few months. She'd come in roughly four years into Morgan's sentence and eventually, the two had grown to be on speaking terms. They'd never really been friends (those were incredibly hard to make in prison, no matter what Hollywood movies claimed) but they'd often shared conversations in the cafeteria, in the gym, or during recreation time.

Kimmy had been arrested for her involvement in a cult. She wasn't sure, but she thought the name of the cult was the Rising Sun of Zion. A lot of what they were involved in was, at its core, based on Christian beliefs. But they took it to the extreme. For instance, Kimmy had been arrested at a rally near an abortion clinic where she'd dumped cow blood on five people and pelted rocks and bricks at police officers who tried to break up the protest. Two of the bricks she threw struck people. She'd knocked one officer unconscious and shattered the elbow of a rival protestor.

While Morgan didn't agree with any of Kimmy's tactics or beliefs, she'd been a fascinating woman to speak to. She'd often make deep dives on what it was like to be in a cult, a topic that Morgan had always found fascinating.

Kimmy always had interesting stories about the Rising Sun of Zion, as well as other cults she'd come into contact with during what she referred to as "her transcendent years." In prison, she'd made a habit of attending Bible studies put on by local churches and completely berating the instructors, bemoaning that Christianity was nothing more than a cult in and of itself.

This wasn't exactly something Morgan believed, but she'd always respected Kimmy for her boldness in the face of her...well, her *unique* approach to things.

Kimmy had described how the cult's rituals were centered around the worship of a supposed messiah who would lead them to a promised land. They saw themselves as the chosen people, and anyone who opposed them was an enemy of the Lord.

Morgan had never understood how someone could become so deluded, so entrenched in their beliefs that they'd be willing to hurt others for it. It was a mystery to her, one that she'd often pondered during her long nights in prison.

Yet somehow, for some reason, she'd never stopped to consider that Samson may be involved in a cult. For all intents and purposes, it seemed like he worked alone. But who was to say he wasn't being sent out as part of a group? And if that was indeed the case, might there be more like Samson also at work elsewhere in the country?

Or, and this was a thought that chilled her to the core, what if the man she was after now wasn't Samson at all? After all, ten years was a hell of a long time to wait. What if this was some other cult member or extremist who had been inspired by Samson's work and was now just finishing it up?

It was an intriguing idea, even if it did feel farfetched. But she wasn't about to ignore any possible answers.

With these new ideas locked in, she regretted the outburst that had destroyed her phone. She could have called Mueller and told him her theory, to convince him to allow her to stay on the case. She felt foolish over the outburst as she parked her car and raced back inside the hospital.

As she took the elevator up to Derik's floor, she did her best to remember some of the names of the other cults Kimmy had mentioned—cults that operated silently and almost unseen in the city and surrounding counties. A few raced through her mind but she wasn't even sure if they were accurate or not.

When she got to Derik's room, she was relieved to see him sitting on the edge of the cushioned table he'd been lying on earlier. A nurse was with him, and he was signing a paper. His discharge papers, Morgan assumed.

"Ma'am," the nurse said, "you can't be in here."

"It's okay," Derik said with a smile. "She's my ride." He handed the nurse the clipboard with the form on it and said, "We good here?"

"Yes, Agent Greene. You're good to go. Don't forget to fill that prescription if you need it. And concussion protocol says you should stay off your feet for a few days."

"I know. Thanks."

"Nurse," Morgan said, "do you think we could have the room for a bit? Maybe five minutes?"

She looked at them skeptically but then shrugged. "Five minutes. But then I'll have to kick you out."

"Thanks."

The nurse left, closing the door behind them. Derik looked at Morgan with curiosity, tilting his head. "What? What's happened?"

"Oh, a lot has happened in the last hour and a half," she said. She then took a deep breath and did her best to summarize it all.

She started with calling Mueller and then the call he'd gotten to inform him of the eleventh victim. She walked him through her visit to Leonard Seabry's residence, and wrapped it up with the destruction of her cell phone. The last thing she told him was about the small epiphany she'd had concerning Kimmy Byers and how she wondered if Samson might be part of a cult.

"Jesus, he worked quick on that last one, huh?"

"We scared him," Morgan said. "I don't think he had a choice."

"I just don't...I don't know why Mueller would do that to you. I guarantee the rest of his little team pushed him to do it."

"You're part of that little team, are you not?"

"Notice I've been here in the time someone made that decision." He sighed, but Morgan could tell he was growing irritated with the situation. "Let me call him. Let me talk to him. I bet I could sway him."

"No, don't do th—"

"How sure are you about this cult theory?"

"I don't know yet, but it feels right," Morgan said. "What about you? What do you think about it?"

Derik leaned back against the wall, rubbing his chin thoughtfully. "It's definitely possible. Cults always seem to operate under the radar until something big happens. And if Samson is part of a group, then there could be more out there just like him."

"Exactly my thoughts."

Cults have been known to operate like that, with one person acting as the 'chosen one' or whatever they call it, and others following blindly in his footsteps."

"So how do we find them?" Morgan asked.

"Well, there's always the internet," Derik said with a smirk.

Morgan rolled her eyes. "I don't have time to sift through conspiracy theories and crackpot websites. And I hate that I can't recall any of the names Kimmy talked about."

"Well, if you'd get out of here and let me call Mueller, I think he can patch me through to records. Someone can hop on the database and give us a few names within minutes."

"Fine," she said. "But if I find out you called and gave him some sob story about me..."

"Nope, I intend to tell him how much of a pain in my ass you're already being. I'm hoping it'll trigger some nostalgia for him."

The smile that came to her face was genuine and took her by surprise. "You won't call him in front of me?"

"Can you keep quiet and not interject or correct me while I talk?"

She shook her head. "Probably not."

"Exactly," Derik said, pointing to the door. "I'll meet you in the downstairs waiting area when I'm done."

Morgan smirked, once again feeling a strange delight that she and Derik were slowly starting to find their footing again. They truly had been a great duo, and it made her embarrassed to realize how badly she'd handled the situation when Mueller had called to take her off of the case.

To bide her time after leaving the room, she took the stairs to the waiting area and grabbed a snack cake from a vending machine. She took a seat on the far side of the room, away from the other three people who sat, tired and anxious to hear about their family members or loved ones. Morgan once again found the comfort of her past, bringing to mind memories of waiting rooms when her mother had been sick.

She also thought of Kimmy Byers again, doing her best to think of some of the other cults she'd mentioned. In Morgan's defense, she sometimes didn't pay much attention to what Kimmy said because once she got going, she started to sound nuts.

She'd nearly finished off her snack when Derik came around the corner and entered the waiting room. He walked over and plopped himself down almost comically into the chair beside her. The wrapping was gone from his head, now replaced with a simple but very bulky bandage that took up most of the left side of his brow.

"Well," he said, "I'll say this. Mueller is pissed off about you hanging up on him. I didn't tell him you trashed the phone, though."

"Thanks, I guess."

"I told him your theory and also told him I thought it would be a smart play to keep you on the case. I got him to agree but I think it's only because he knows you have the badge and the gun. If someone higher up got wind of how quickly he'd pulled you after making the decision to put you on the case, it would look bad for him."

"Makes sense."

"He did say he's not comfortable with you having a sidearm, though. So I've been tasked with keeping a close eye on you."

Morgan nodded, biting back a smile. "And there you go again...believing in me when no one else does."

"I know. I'm pretty great. Anyway, Mueller also has Records and Research assembling a collection of known, active cults in the area. While we wait for that to come through, I'd like to grab something to eat. And maybe switch out this ridiculous bandage. This thing itches like crazy."

"Mueller was okay with you heading out with the injury?"

Derik shrugged and said, "I may have downplayed it a bit."

"But are you actually okay?"

"I think so," he said, getting to his feet. He gestured for her to follow him. "Come on. Let's see."

Morgan was slightly uncomfortable with this but got up anyway. She knew Derik wouldn't put a case in jeopardy. If he was really hurt, there was no way he'd keep going.

So she followed him out of the waiting room and out into the parking lot. Morgan felt like she was stuck in a loop, as she'd walked through the same doors, out into the same parking lot, less than two hours earlier. The day was coming to a close and she somehow felt that if they didn't catch their killer before the next day started, he'd get away. She had no facts or actual clues on which this was based; it was just a gut feeling that she couldn't ignore.

But with her and Derik starting to recapture some of that old camaraderie that had once existed between them, she thought they had a pretty good chance of capturing Samson even if he was done with his work.

CHAPTER EIGHTEEN

Because of Derik's head injury, Morgan elected to drive. She was surprised at how much she enjoyed it after having been locked away for a decade. There was an immense freedom in the act that she'd always overlooked and taken for granted—a much larger freedom than the one she'd felt while sitting in the passenger seat earlier.

She drove to Derik's fast-food restaurant of choice and they both grabbed burgers and sodas. As they waited for the man at the drive-thru window to hand them their late lunch, Derik spoke up from the passenger seat.

"Wow...that was fast. Mueller must really want this thing knocked out."

"What is it?" Morgan asked as she took the bag of food. She glanced over to Derik and saw that he was looking at something on his phone.

"A complete list of all known cults in the area and the crimes they've committed or been linked to." He frowned as he thumbed through the email. "It's surprisingly brief."

"How many?"

"Just four. And one is indeed the one you mentioned to me. The Rising Sun of Zion. But the only crimes I see them connected with are little acts of violence at the occasional protests and outside of churches."

"Okay," Morgan said as she pulled out of the drive-thru lane and into the first available parking space she could find. "What else is on the list?"

Derik scrolled down on his phone, his face furrowed in concentration. "The second one is the Children of the Serpent. They're a small group that's mainly focused on spreading their beliefs through social media. They haven't been linked to any crimes, but they do have a history of harassment and cyberbullying."

"What's their belief system?" Morgan asked, taking a bite of her burger.

"From what I can tell, they seem to be a mix of new age spirituality and conspiracy theories. They believe in things like reptilian overlords and the Illuminati controlling the world."

Morgan rolled her eyes. "Sounds like a bunch of winners. Who else?"

"Just two more. This one is a bit of a wildcard. They call themselves the Children of Orpheus. They're a musical cult, believe it or not. They claim to be devoted to the Greek god of music and poetry, but they've been known to do some pretty bizarre things during their shows."

"Like what?" Morgan asked, intrigued.

"Um...it says here, orgies on stage. So the few dings with the police have all been related to public indecency. But here...this last one...this one sounds more like what we're looking for. The Order of the Black Star. They're a bit more elusive but they've been tied to a few cases of arson and vandalism. There are also three cases of assault and one case of attempted murder."

"Do we have a name for the murder attempt?" Morgan asked. She was a bit distracted by her burger, too, though. God, she'd missed a good burger.

"We do. Randall Easterly. And because this is a list for just the cults, I don't have an address for him."

"Do you have one for where the group meets?"

"I do."

He wolfed down the last of his burger as he plugged the address into his phone. Using the maps app, he directed Morgan to the address. Morgan could tell within the first few turns that they were being led to the outskirts of the city, on the opposite side of the river and the mines they'd explored earlier in the day.

"Hey," Derik said. "Remember earlier when you made me tell you about one of my most exciting work moments while you were out?"

"Yes, but I believe I referred to it as a case...not a work moment."

"Whatever. Would you do that for me?"

"Do what?"

"Tell me something about prison...but not anything bad. Tell me one thing that you actually enjoyed."

She almost told him this was a stupid idea but she also understood what he was doing. He was trying to center her, to ground her. He wanted her to face the ten years that hung over their heads like an anvil, but in a way that was positive.

So she thought about it for a moment and then, with a smile on her face, gave her best answer.

"The library."

Derik raised an eyebrow. "The library?"

Morgan nodded. "Yeah. I mean, of course it wasn't as big or as varied as a public library, but it was still a place where I could lose myself in a book. And it was quiet. There was no yelling or fighting or anything. Just me, a book, and peace and quiet."

Derik nodded understandingly. "I get it. Sometimes it's the little things that matter. And you did always like to read."

She almost stopped there, though she did have one more thing to tell about the library. She decided to share it with him because it was something she had been excited to share with her father. But now that her dad was gone, she figured she should share it with someone, no matter how silly it seemed.

"Believe it or not, I learned how to knit because of a few of the books in the library," Morgan said, remembering the countless hours spent with needles and yarn. "It was a skill I never thought I'd pick up, but it was so calming and therapeutic. Plus, I made some pretty cute scarves."

Derik chuckled. "I never would have guessed. Knitting doesn't really seem like your thing."

"Well, it wasn't until I had to spend every day for years with nothing but my thoughts," Morgan replied. "You learn to try new things to keep your mind occupied."

Derik nodded. "I can imagine. But, still…knitting?"

"Yes. And if you keep poking fun, I won't give you the scarf I made you."

"You made me a scarf?"

"Sort of," she said, starting to get embarrassed.

Derik smiled as the subject was dropped.

As they drew closer to the address, Morgan realized she knew exactly where they were headed. Early in her career, she'd responded to a case on the property in question. It was a strange-looking building, situated in a wooded lot about a mile down a gravel road.

Still, the place seemed strange and slightly creepy as she guided the car down the gravel road. The trees on either side loomed large and gloomy, casting deep shadows over the car and the road. The road itself was a long, winding path that took them deep into the woods before finally opening up into a small clearing, where the cult's building stood. It was a tall, narrow structure, with a steeply pitched roof and dark, forbidding windows that seemed to stare back at them.

Morgan parked the car next to a small shed, which was the only other structure in the clearing, and she and Derik got out to take a closer look at the building. There were a few other cars parked in the dusty little parking lot. Three people were currently exiting a small car, heading for the building's front doors. One of them looked over at Morgan and Derik, giving them a small nod.

"Seems like we're just in time for...well, for something," Derik said.

This became even more apparent as they got close to the tall, heavy front door, which was made of a dark wood. Morgan could hear voices chanting from inside, and it sent a shiver down her spine. One of the three ahead of them politely held the door open for them. So far, Morgan thought it was like attending a typical church service, only at three in the afternoon on a Thursday.

They stepped inside with the group of three and found themselves standing in a small entryway. There was a large desk sitting against the wall to the right. A piece of paper on a clipboard served as a sign-in sheet. Beside it were three stacks of sleek, black robes. Directly ahead of them was another large wooden door. This one was open, revealing a larger room on the other side. Morgan looked over the shoulders of the group ahead of them and she could see eight people dressed in the robes, standing in two lines and facing one another.

Morgan watched as each of the three people ahead of them took a robe and slid it on. They then signed the paper at the desk and as they did, Morgan noted a very serious expression on each of their faces. They certainly seemed as if they'd done this before. Morgan assumed a group such as the Order of the Black Star wasn't big on attracting new followers.

"You sure about this?" Morgan asked, whispering to Derik.

He nodded and picked up one of the robes.

Morgan followed suit, taking a deep breath as she slipped the black fabric over her clothes. The material was smooth, almost silky to the touch, and it made her feel uneasy for reasons she couldn't quite explain. She couldn't shake off the feeling that this was a bad idea. But they were here now, so there was no sense in turning back.

As they approached the open door to the larger room, Morgan could hear the chanting growing louder. She could now see that the robed figures had formed a circle. The room was dimly lit with a few flickering candles, and the air was thick with incense.

Morgan tried to remain as inconspicuous as possible, but she couldn't shake the feeling of unease that settled in her stomach. This only increased when she saw two of the people who had already been inside the room staring at her and Derik. One member, a gorgeous brunette who wore a hood over her head, attached to the robe, made no effort to hide the fact that she was staring them down with scorn.

But before the moment could get any more tense, the sound of a door opening caught everyone's attention. Everyone turned to the back of the room, where another robed figure entered through a darkened doorway. His robe was not black like everyone else's but a dark shade of red, nearly maroon. He carried a single candle, which he brought to the group. Those who had created a circle parted a bit to allow him room.

He placed the candle on the floor, in the center of the group, and then the circle closed in again. Morgan had to remind herself that she was trying to play a part and did her best to stay in the circle. Derik seemed a bit more aware of the part he was supposed to be playing and joined it without any hesitancy.

The man in the red robe—the leader, Morgan assumed—stepped to the top portion of the circle. It was a position that nearly set him and Morgan up to be directly across from one another. He scanned the circle of people and as his eyes found Morgan, she tilted her head downward a bit.

Seconds later, the red-robed man spoke. His voice was sultry, soothing, and quite deep.

"Greetings, members of the Order of the Black Star," he said. "Today we will, as always, commune and talk of things both sacred and holy. We will speak of community and of the Seven Signs."

Those last two words grabbed Morgan so fiercely that she almost completely missed what came next—a comment that caused her heart to sink and a spike of fear to tear right through it.

"First, however, we must deal with the reckoners among us," he said. "False tongues and snakes, make yourselves known or I will call you out."

And when Morgan looked back at him, she was not at all surprised to see that the red-robed man was looking directly at her and Derik.

CHAPTER NINETEEN

No one spoke, but every set of eyes in the room was now on Morgan and Derik. Morgan hated the feeling; it wasn't too dissimilar to being outside on a sweaty day and feeling gnats swarming her skin.

Morgan did not see the point in feigning ignorance. All of the members were looking at them, after all. And she figured if they could go ahead and address them logically, this whole ordeal may turn out easier than she'd hoped.

"We're not reckoners, and we certainly aren't snakes," Morgan said. "We are here because we've heard of your Order and were curious." She figured she'd wait to reveal who they truly were when they were completely out of options. No sense in causing unnecessary panic.

"She's right," Derik said. "We just had no idea how to go about being invited."

"You aren't invited into the Order of the Black Star," the leader said. "You are recruited."

"How?" Morgan asked.

"If you don't know, you have no business here."

"You mentioned the Seven Signs," Morgan said, ignoring his little jab. "Can you tell us how your Order approaches that?"

"No." It was a simple response without anger or urgency.

"Can you tell us what the Order of the Black Star believes?"

The leader arched an eyebrow at Morgan's question, his gaze piercing through her. "That is something only those of us in the Order know," he said. "It is not for outsiders to understand."

Morgan could feel her frustration growing, but she managed to keep her demeanor calm. "I understand," she said. "But we're genuinely interested in learning more about your beliefs. Is there anything you can tell us?"

The leader's eyes narrowed as he studied Morgan and Derik for a moment. In that gaze, she was quite sure he knew she was lying...that they had no real interest in their Order.

Then, almost out of the blue, the leader answered. It sounded rehearsed, but with each word he spoke, Morgan became more certain that this was very likely where Samson had gotten his start. Hell, maybe he was even still a member.

Or, for that matter, maybe Samson was the man standing in front of her.

"We believe in enlightenment, in breaking free from societal constraints and discovering the true nature of the self. We believe in the power of the occult and the magical arts. And we believe in the Seven Signs, the divine omens that herald the coming of the end times."

Morgan felt a chill flush through her. This was exactly what Samson believed…what had driven him to kill eleven people.

The next question out of her mouth came before she could stop it. The answers they'd received so far had pushed her to the edge, and she was done screwing around in this silly robe, pretending to be interested in this nonsense.

"Do you know a man named Samson?" she asked. She gauged his reaction carefully.

"You can't know our names," the leader said. "Not without at least revealing your true identity first."

"My true identity?" she asked, anger and annoyance creeping into her voice. "You want to know my true identity?"

She could hear Derik beside her, whispering: "Careful, Morgan…"

She reached into her robe and before she could pull her badge and ID, four of the members moved out of the circle. They quickly created a protective wall of bodies around their red-robed leader.

They remained that way when she showed her badge. "We're Agents Cross and Greene, with the FBI. We need to ask you some questions regarding the Seven Signs."

The leader spoke up from behind the wall of four members. The others were scattered to the side, as if they had no idea what to do. "Pretending to come in as members and faking an interest in what we do is no way to go about that."

"Well, we'll go about it this way, then. We need to speak with you."

"I'm afraid not. You're infringing on our religious freedoms. And we're right in the middle of a ritual service."

"Well, it's just going to have to wait."

"I think not. Be smart, Agent. Federal agents infiltrating a very small place of worship and making demands. Do you know how the headlines will look?"

"I don't care about that. I've got eleven dead people and a killer that's been very patient in making sure we're aware that he's always one step ahead."

"Morgan..." Derik said again, giving a cautious warning.

"And if I say no, do you intend to arrest me? Is that how it's going to go?"

"It just might."

"Then fine. Let's see you do it."

Morgan didn't even hesitate. She started forward, fueled by anger and frustration. But as she neared the leader, a man she thought could be Samson after all, given his arrogance, the wall of four members stepped forward to stop her.

"Excuse me," she said, giving the first one—a man of about thirty or so—a small nudge.

When she nudged him, he shoved her arm away. And when Morgan reacted to this, she knew she was overreacting but was helpless to stop herself. She had ten years pent up, ten years of frustration and anxiousness that was begging to come out.

She captured the man's arm as he pushed at her. As he let out a cry of surprise, Morgan turned slightly to the right and brought his arm over in a downward motion as she dipped at the waist. The result was an effective hip toss that sent the man hurtling into the members of the wall next to him.

As the other two came rushing at Morgan, Derik drew his Glock. Morgan saw this happen, but just barely. Because in that same moment, the remaining members scattered. Two went rushing for the back doors, one of whom was screaming. Another ran for the back door, and the other two members of the little human wall stood in place. One even raised their hands slightly into the air.

During it all, one of the remaining members of what had once been a circle took the leader by the arm and also made their way for the door at the back.

"Nope!" Morgan called, reaching for her own Glock. "Hold it right there!"

"Morgan, for God's sake..." Derik said. "Careful!"

She recalled how he'd told her Mueller expressed that he should keep an eye on her. And in that moment, she knew he was right to be concerned. There was just so much anger coursing through her, so much aggravation. Grunting in frustration, she holstered her Glock and took off at a run. Behind her, Derik was following, his Glock still out.

But he was running with the awkward control of a man who had just been released from the hospital with a concussion.

As the leader and his escort reached the doorway, there was a brief breath of a moment where they had to pause, the escort allowing the leader to go through first. And that was all the window Morgan needed.

She body-checked the escort into the doorframe. There was the cracking sound of wood splitting as the man's body rebounded hard. He tumbled and went to the ground as Morgan hurried through the doorway. The room beyond was dark, lit by only a few candles. But she could see the shape of the leader (Samson, she told herself...there's a very good chance that's Samson) racing through the room.

He looked back to see where she was, and that was his mistake. It slowed him just enough for Morgan to close in. She reached out as they ran, grabbing a handful of cloak. Morgan planted her feet, locked her knees, and yanked her arm back with the robe still clutched in her hand.

The leader made a choking sound as the robe rightened around his neck. As he stumbled backward, Morgan caught him, locking an arm behind his back as she instantly wheeled him back around to the door.

"Your fucking head will roll for this!" the leader roared.

"We'll see," she said as she wrestled him back through the door.

Derik was slowly coming forward, removing his handcuffs from his belt, and coming with the assist. As she cuffed the leader, Morgan noticed that he wasn't putting up a fight. He was standing perfectly still and not resisting at all.

In a way, it seemed like he wanted this to happen. And as far as Morgan was concerned, that was the scariest thing of all.

CHAPTER TWENTY

There was an overwhelming sense of tension when Morgan and Derik entered the field office. As she and Derik escorted the leader of the Order of the Black Star through the main floor's back corridor to the interrogation rooms, Morgan knew it was only a matter of time before AD Mueller would show up. And rightfully so; she'd had a bit of a temper tantrum, and Derik had suffered a blow to the head.

Also, there was a chance that a case ten years in the making was coming to a close...that the killer of eleven people was currently under their roof.

As it turned out, they didn't have to wait for Mueller. He and Assistant Director Yen were standing at the entrance to the hallway that held the interrogation rooms.

"This is him?" Mueller asked as they approached the door to the first interrogation room.

"Could be," Morgan said. "We need to question him, of course."

Mueller then turned his attention to Derik and cringed a bit. "Jesus, Greene. Are you okay?"

"Been better."

It wasn't until Morgan opened the door and led the leader inside that she realized Mueller fully intended to go in as well. She handed the leader off to Derik and then turned to Mueller. In a voice barely above a whisper, she said, "Can I speak with you outside?"

"Quickly," he said.

They walked back out into the hallway, where Yen still waited. Mueller leaned against the wall and looked expectantly at Morgan. Apparently, he knew what was coming and wasn't going to make this easy.

"I'm sorry I hung up on you earlier," she said. "If you want the full truth, yeah...maybe it was a mistake for me to jump back on this so soon. But you have to let me see this through. I've waited for ten years..."

"I know you did. And I should have let that be the most important thing. But when that next victim popped up just days before your release...we all freaked out. It became abundantly clear that you had nothing to do with...well, with what we thought you did all those years ago. And we wanted the case wrapped before the media got their hooks into it." He nodded to the door to the interrogation room and added: "And it seems like we may have done that. The deaths will hit the news, sure, but the fact that we have the bastard already certainly helps."

"So we're good?"

"Yes. I do think once this is a wrap, you need to take some time to get acclimated to your life again. If you'll accept my apology for jumping the gun, I'll gladly accept yours."

"Agreed…if you'll let me and Derik wrap this. If this is our guy, I don't want him swamped with too many agents. If it's him, I think he'll talk easily enough if it's just me."

Mueller considered it for a moment and then nodded. "Fine. Go on in and see what you can get from him. But I want updates as soon as humanly possible."

"Sounds good," Morgan said. She gave a little nod of appreciation and then entered the interrogation room again.

The leader, whom she was now trying her best to think of as Samson, was sitting behind the gleaming, fake-wood desk. His hands were still cuffed as he looked up at Morgan and Derik with a great deal of patience.

"Do you know why we brought you in here?" she asked, hoping to break the ice.

The man nodded. "I have an idea."

"Would you be willing to tell us why you think we brought you in here?"

"You seemed interested in the Seven Signs. I assume it has something to do with the murders."

She sat on this for a while, looking at Derik. She didn't want to reveal too much because if this was indeed Samson, it would take away many of the traps she could verbally set for him during the rest of the interrogation.

"That's correct," she said. "What's your name?"

The man chuckled, looking at her as if she were an idiot. "You mean to tell me that you arrested me without even knowing my name?"

"Samson."

The man thought about this for a moment and ended up not answering at all. "Tell me what you know about the Seven Signs," he said instead.

"No."

"Fine, then. Tell me...do you really think a mortal man can kill people in order to bring about the return of a messiah?"

"No, I don't," Morgan said.

"Same," Derik echoed.

"Nor do I," the man said. "I am very aware of the murders you are investigating, but I am not this Samson you are looking for. We know what he is doing...what he thinks the end result will be. And it disgusts us."

"Can you prove you're not Samson?" Morgan asked.

She watched him closely. When the look of confusion and then sheer amusement crossed his face, she knew they had the wrong man. And it was also in that moment that she realized she'd made a careless mistake. It was a mistake she would not have made ten years ago. But her instincts were rusty, and she'd been attacking this case with far too much personal emotion to think logically.

She thought of the doorbell camera back at Leonard Seabry's house. All she needed to do was look at that footage. Even if the killer was somehow covering his face, she could probably still tell if it was the man sitting in front of her.

Shit, she thought.

"Do you know anyone by that name?" Derik asked. Apparently, he'd also come to the same conclusion Morgan had. She could hear the faint traces of disappointment in his voice.

"I can't say that I do." A thin smile crept onto his face as he seemed to understand what was going on. "You think...you think I'm the killer? You think I'm your Seven Signs Killer?"

Morgan nearly asked how he knew about the Seven Signs Killer, but she then reminded herself that it had been all over the news before she'd gone to prison. She could only assume there had been countless news articles, conspiracy theories, and stories written about it during her time away.

"That was the speculation, yes," Morgan said. "And when we heard you reference the Seven Signs, that was more than enough for us to ask to speak with you....which you did not handle well."

"I handled it perfectly well. I know my rights, Agent Cross."

"Are the Seven Signs you mentioned in reference to the Seven Signs of Christ?"

"They are. But not bound by the almost legalistic restrictions of the Bible."

"What does the Order of the Black Star do?"

He sighed here, that little smirk still on his face. "Well, we don't kill people, I can tell you that right now. At most, we have killed small animals."

"As a means of a sacrifice?" Derik asked.

"Yes. Wild animals. Not pets. Not anything illegal. We always make sure of that."

Morgan knew a good deal about biblical teaching because of her father. She was quite sure there was nothing about killing small animals in reverence of Christ. There was plenty of killing in the Old Testament, taking animals to the altar for God, but very little, if any, in the New Testament after Christ came along.

"What are these sacrifices for?" Morgan asked.

"We seek to purify ourselves," he replied. "To rid ourselves of our fleshly desires and become more like Christ. The animals are simply vessels through which we can symbolically offer ourselves as sacrifices to God. It is also our way of accepting death and opening our minds to the idea of resurrection. That is the only real reverence we hold toward the Seven Signs. We do not seek to walk on water, for example. We only seek to find a way to accept and perhaps even avoid a permanent spiritual death."

Morgan could feel her frustration growing. This man was clearly not their killer, and yet she couldn't shake the feeling that he knew more than he was letting on.

"Is there anything else you can tell us about the Seven Signs or the Order of the Black Star?" she asked.

He shook his head. "Nothing that I'm sure you don't already know. I can see in your eyes that you know I am not the man you're looking for. Now…I've said all I'm willing to say. Am I free to go?"

"One more thing," Morgan said, starting to feel desperate now. "We believe that our Seven Signs Killer began his so-called work because he either believes himself to be the messiah or he is attempting to, in his skewed way, roll out the red carpet for the return of Christ. Does that sound like anything at all the Order of the Black Star believes?"

The thin smile on his face finally disappeared and he looked rather grim. "Absolutely not. To think anything we do can influence the decisions of an all-powerful God is close to blasphemy. Based on that alone, I can assure you that our killer is in no way affiliated with the Order."

"Thank you," Morgan said. "Now, for the sake of making paperwork easier on not only the bureau, but yourself as well, I need your name. We need you to stay here anyway, while we check alibis and a few other things." She once again thought about the doorbell footage and how that might further prove this man's innocence.

The leader looked angry for a moment but then seemed to relax a bit, resigning himself to his fate. "Fine. I'm Christopher Newman. I've been the Chief Priest of the Dallas–Fort Worth branch of the Order of the Black Star for three years now."

"And if we asked you for alibis over the last several days, would you be able to provide them?"

"Yes. That won't be a problem. I do intend to file several complaints about what went down today."

"Knock yourself out," Morgan said, turning her back and heading for the door.

Back out in the hallway, Mueller was waiting. When Morgan realized Derik wasn't quite ready to leave Christopher Newman just yet, she closed the door. *Maybe*, she thought, *he's going to start fishing for alibis.*

"Well?" Mueller said.

"I'm almost positive he's not our killer."

"How do you know?"

"Because his cult and the leanings of our killer…the belief systems don't line up. I think once we get alibis and I check a few things from Leonard Seabry's residence, we'll know for sure."

Mueller placed his hands on his hips and sighed deeply. "So what happens now? If this man isn't our killer and nothing checks out at Seabry's place, what's your next step?"

She felt like he was quizzing her. She felt that if she gave a wrong response, he'd try pulling her from the case again.

"I'm not sure yet. But…the more I think about it, the more I'm not so sure this latest victim means he's done."

"What makes you think that?"

"Call it a hunch."

"I can't go on that. Morgan, look…I'm going to speak candidly, okay?"

"Okay."

"I do still feel you're the best agent for this. I can only imagine how much time you spent thinking about it for the past ten years. But I also know that ten years away from this job is a lifetime. I know you're rusty. I know your instincts aren't as sharp as they used to be. And some of that is…well, some of that is my fault. I know I didn't do enough to keep you out."

"I'm not trying to assign blame," she said. This was true...now. But she'd spent about her first year or so behind bars doing just that.

"Well, I mention all of that to say that my gut is telling me to trust you on this. If you don't think this guy is our killer, I'm good with that. But his alibis have to be very solid. And what was it you wanted to check at Seabry's?"

"Footage from the doorbell camera. It'll rule this guy out...name is Christopher Newman, by the way."

Mueller nodded, seemingly satisfied with the direction. "Alright. I'll get started on getting Newman's alibis and checking out Seabry's place. You and Derik keep doing what you're doing. Speaking of...do you think Derik is fit to work? That blow to the head..."

She thought of how Derik's call to Mueller earlier had smoothed things over. She had to reciprocate.

"I think it was bothering him at first, but he seems fine now. I think he's feeling like me. There's just...this overwhelming feeling that we're at the end, but it's not over. We're just waiting for..."

She stopped there, her mind locking down on that one word.

Waiting.

This entire time, they'd been searching for the Seven Signs Killer, thinking he was enacting these signs in order to bring about the end of the world...to pave the way for the return of a messiah.

His work was done. Now all he had left to do was wait. And if he'd done all of his killing here, in the Dallas–Fort Worth area, he certainly wouldn't leave. No, he'd stay nearby. He'd want to herald in the messiah.

But how? Where?

And in that moment, she thought she knew. It might be a long shot, but it felt right.

She opened the door to the interrogation room and looked at Derik. He was speaking to Christopher Newman, working on the man's alibis.

"AD Mueller has volunteered to work on the alibis," she said. And then, with a sting of pity, she added: "And I think you need to stay here with him. I saw you staggering back at the Black Star building."

Derik frowned, clearly knowing she was right. He ran a hand along the bandage on his head as if to make sure it was still there. "But I'm supposed to keep an eye on you, remember?"

"Well, what if I promise to be very careful and to play by the rules?"

"Then I'd call you a liar."

"Fair enough. I can live with that."

"Do you at least want to tell me where you're going?"

She almost did but decided not to. If he knew what she had in mind, he'd insist on going along. "Not yet. It may pan out to be nothing anyway."

"Just be careful. I do remember how you tend to jump into things without looking ahead."

She smiled. It was a pretty accurate summary of how she tended to act when the pressure was on.

"I have no idea what you're talking about."

With that, she turned and hurried back down the hallway. She was certain either Derik or Mueller would call out to her, to make her stop. But she made it out the door without incident, and by the time she made it to the parking lot, Morgan was practically running toward the car.

CHAPTER TWENTY ONE

The visit to the Order of the Black Star was what brought everything full circle for Morgan. Christopher Newman had referred to what they'd been in the midst of as a ritual. Morgan had no idea what sort of ritual it might have been, but that wasn't important.

The word *ritual* was what had clued Morgan in.

From the very beginning of this case, by the time Samson's second victim had been claimed, he'd left little letters and clues to indicate that he was doing his gruesome business as a way to bring forth a messiah, to welcome an entity that would wash the world anew and bring a new beginning.

From Morgan's FBI agent perspective, though, she'd simply seen the case as nothing more than a series of murders...interconnected deaths that were all tied to one single, deranged killer.

But she wondered if killing all of those people under the shadow of the Seven Signs made it something more...something resembling a ritual. All the signs and approaches were there, after all.

As she drove to the location she suspected might lead her to Samson and, hopefully, the end of this case—after a quick stop to buy a new burner phone—she viewed the case under this new filter. What if these event deaths, all undertaken for a particular reason, were part of a ritual of sorts? How did that change the case?

If this was a ritual and Samson was expecting a certain outcome, certainly he had a final place in mind...some area where he expected the messiah to arrive. And based on the new information she'd accumulated on the case since getting out of prison, she thought she knew where that location might be.

She was headed back for the mines. It was the one location where they'd actually gotten the jump on Samson. He'd seemed just as surprised at them showing up as they'd been to find him there. From what Morgan could tell, the site held some sort of significance to him. And while his knowledge of the system of tunnels and caves obviously gave him an advantage, it wasn't enough to keep Morgan away.

Of course, she could be totally wrong. Maybe his cave system had simply been a hiding spot of sorts...a place he would definitely not return to now that the bureau knew he'd been there.

But if the location was essential to his ritual, it seemed almost a certainty that he'd return. And that was the chance Morgan was taking now, as she headed for the old mines.

As she drove, Morgan's mind raced with different scenarios of what she might find at the mines. She considered every angle, thinking about how Samson could have set up the area to welcome the messiah, or how he might have planned to use the tunnels to make his final move.

After all, she and Derik had only glimpsed a small portion of the tunnels. There was no telling what else was waiting in the dusty bends and folds of those pathways.

She considered the idea of calling for backup, but she already knew Mueller hadn't trusted her original hunch to come to these mines. If she called and told him where she was and what she intended to do, he'd not only *not* send backup, but he'd chew her out over the phone.

So she was going to have to do this alone.

When the bridge came into view, Morgan realized that she barely even remembered the drive. She'd been so locked in, so targeted in on her end goal of bringing this to an end. Capturing Samson suddenly seemed like the most important thing in the world. It would not only bring a known killer to justice, but it would end this terrible chapter of her life. In a strange and skewed way, Morgan thought it might almost make the ten years in prison worth it.

Almost.

Finally, she arrived at the area where she and Derik had parked earlier. She locked the car and stepped out into the little field they'd walked across roughly seven hours ago. She found the little trail that wound down closer to the river. It felt a bit more treacherous now that she was there by herself and with dusk descending all around her. The trail led her back to the same spot, coming around the bend and escorting her to the small washed-away spot that served as the entrance.

Morgan took a deep breath and approached the entrance of the mines. Her heart was pounding in her chest, and she could feel a bead of sweat trickling down the side of her face. She knew that if Samson was here, things could turn ugly very quickly. What had happened to Derik earlier in the day was proof of this.

She squeezed in with the same difficulty as before, between the barricade and barrier. As she made her way into the darkness, gripping the flashlight she'd brought with her very tightly, she wondered if Samson had some other way to get inside. Coming in and out this way more than a few times would be maddening.

Probably, she thought. It was another reminder that he apparently had an almost intimate knowledge of these mines.

She knew she'd been standing there earlier in the day, but nothing about the place looked familiar. Yet, at the same time, parts of it were almost welcoming. Maybe it was the darkness, playing tricks on her mind and eyes. She figured the only thing she could do was venture farther inside and hope she started to remember things.

Sure enough, she did. It took about ten minutes, but she eventually came to the place where Derik had been hit. The small chamber just up ahead on the right served as a marker of sorts. She shone her light into it and saw the same setup as before. A few candles and small indications that the room had recently been in use.

She then redirected herself. She had to fight to trust her instincts, but she eventually found the route Samson had taken when he'd made a run for it. After a few more minutes, she found herself in the tunnel where she'd had to make that terrible decision: continue chasing Samson, or head back to make sure Derik was okay.

As she walked, she encountered several forks in the tunnel, and it took all her concentration to remember which way she had come from so that she didn't loop back around. She couldn't afford to get lost down here, not with the stakes so high.

The walls seemed to shrink, growing in tighter and tighter around her. Each time she came to a new bend or branch, she shone her flashlight around the area, trying to see if there was any movement in the darkness. But there was nothing. No sound, no movement, nothing to indicate that Samson was anywhere nearby.

She had no idea how long she'd been down there. Maybe forty minutes at most. It was long enough for her to consider the fact that maybe she was wrong. Maybe these mines weren't as important to Samson as she'd originally thought.

The mines were quiet, but as she kept going, she could hear the sound of water dripping from the ceiling. She shone her flashlight around the area, and that was when she heard it—a soft, almost inaudible chanting coming from the room ahead.

A single male voice, speaking into the darkness.

And then she saw a flickering light source ahead, dancing weakly in the shadows.

Morgan's heart began to race as she approached the source of the chanting. She knew she was getting close to Samson, and the thought of finally capturing him made her feel alive. She moved quietly, trying to make as little noise as possible. She didn't want to alert Samson to her presence just yet.

As she approached the source of the light, she saw that it was coming from a small room. The chanting was getting louder, and she could now make out some of the words. It was a prayer of some sort, but she couldn't quite make out what it was for.

Morgan's hand went to her gun, but she hesitated. She knew that if she were to make a move now, it could be disastrous. Samson was dangerous, and she didn't want to risk anything.

She took a deep breath and slowly made her way to the entrance of the room. She peeked inside and saw a small altar made of rocks and bones. Candles flickered around it, casting eerie shadows on the walls. She stepped into the chamber, her hand hovering over her Glock.

"Samson," she said. She didn't have to ask. She already knew. He was here somewhere.

Just not in this room. He was close, though. She could hear him chanting. Of course, she could only imagine the sort of tricks these mines and tunnels would play on sound. He could still be a good distance away, but if the acoustics of these tunnels were at all misleading, it could sound as if he were right on top of her.

Frustrated and just a little spooked, Morgan continued into the room. She saw a thin, yet tall opening along the back of the chamber, right where two walls intersected. And as she walked over to it, she saw another small light source coming from within.

Morgan approached the opening cautiously, shining her flashlight inside. It was a tight squeeze, but she knew she had to see what was inside. She squeezed through the opening and found herself in a small chamber. The chanting was louder now, and she knew she was getting closer.

She followed the sound of the chanting and came to another opening. She was looking into another chamber right away, yet another opening to her right. And the moment she saw this, the chanting came to a stop.

The mines went eerily quiet. Morgan focused on that silence, listening for any signs of movement. She still heard that dripping noise further back and, layered with it, a very soft sound. Like the footsteps of someone trying to sneak around.

Fear seized her as she finally drew her Glock. The sudden silence told her that Samson knew she was here...that he was on to her and using his knowledge of this tunnel system to get the drop on her. She didn't want to be stuck in a tunnel if he did manage to get the best of her, so she made her way into the next little room instead.

Another tiny altar sat at the back, a single candle flickering just like the chamber before. She realized that there were three different openings all around here...three different ways for Samson to get to her. She leveled the flashlight, scanning the room with her left hand while she held the Glock in her right.

She stood in the dark, heart hammering madly in her chest, waiting.

Suddenly, she heard a faint rustling from one of the openings. She quickly turned toward the sound, pointing her gun at the opening. But she saw nothing. The rustling had stopped.

Morgan took a few deep breaths, trying to calm her nerves. She knew she had to be careful. Samson was dangerous, and she couldn't afford to make a mistake.

Just then, she heard footsteps coming from behind her. She quickly spun, ready to point her gun at the sound. But it was too late. Samson had already grabbed her from behind, wrapping his arm around her neck. His grip was instantly like a vise. She was quite sure both arms were wrapped around her neck as he pulled her back. They struck one of the walls, an intended action by Samson, as he tightened his grip around her neck. She tried to fight against him, but it only served to cut off her air supply.

Morgan struggled, trying to break free, but Samson was too strong. She felt his hot breath on her neck, and she knew he was enjoying this.

"You wasted ten years of your life in prison because of things I did," he whispered in her ear. "And this is how it ends. You should have just stayed in prison."

Morgan gritted her teeth, trying to hold on to consciousness as Samson tightened his grip. She knew she was in trouble. Yes, she had a Glock, but firing it blindly out into the darkness in such a tight space, with rock walls to all sides, could prove very dangerous.

"It's not over for you yet, though," he said. His voice was starting to sound far away. And even though the little chamber was dark all around her, she could sense everything fading...her thoughts, her hearing, everything.

To hell with it, she thought.

She started to raise the Glock, trying to angle it so that it would turn at a backward slant. But as she raised it, the strength went out of her arm as her lungs begged for air. And then, just as she thought her chest might collapse from the lack of air, Samson released her.

He'd timed it perfectly. Her knees swayed and she felt her head grow light, as if it were swimming away. And at that, Morgan fell and faded away herself, feeling as if the darkness of the mines had swallowed her up.

CHAPTER TWENTY TWO

He looked down at her body, motionless but still breathing on the chamber floor. She was quite pretty but he could tell she was hollow inside. Something about her was missing. He knew she'd been locked away from the world for a decade…the result of a very messy situation pertaining to the fourth victim.

He recalled what she'd looked like ten years ago. She'd been so fast, so determined…a worthwhile opponent. But based on what he'd seen this last couple of days, most of that was gone now. All that was left was rage and a muted sort of obsession.

But in all honesty, that was good. It would make what needed to happen next even more poetic.

She and her partner had known this entire time that he was working to fulfill testaments of the Seven Signs. But what they had likely missed was there was one last sign…one that would ensure the coming of the messiah.

That final sign wasn't so much a sign as it was a sacrifice. In the same way Christ had died upon the cross for the sake of all mankind, someone else would have to die to usher in the coming of the messiah.

And the last name of the woman at his feet just seemed like a delicious little irony. And once she was dead, the messiah would indeed come back. No matter how often he thought back to when he'd started his work, Samson could not recall the exact moment he knew that Morgan Cross was going to have her part to play in this.

He felt it was after he'd enacted the Second Sign. He'd watched the police and feds come and go through the window of a diner at the end of the same block he'd taken the life. Morgan had caught his attention right away and, though he knew it would be foolish, he'd followed her for a while after that. He'd studied her movements, her daily routines. He'd watched her come and go with her partner, watched how diligently she had pursued the case, how badly she'd wanted to find him.

He had chosen her for the last kill because he respected her. And also, saving the strongest sacrifice for last seemed more pleasing.

He knew this. He felt it. He could recall with perfect clarity when this message had first come to him—when he'd been called to enact the Seven Signs and summon the messiah forward.

He had been in a similar situation, standing over the body of a woman he had just killed. But instead of feeling guilt or remorse, he had felt a sudden clarity. He knew what he had to do. He knew that he was meant to bring about the end of the world and the beginning of a new age.

The first victim had felt...well, it had felt like practice. And in the moment immediately following that woman's death, he'd known. He'd known it was only the beginning...that much more death was to come. And that it was all for good reason.

And now, standing in this small chamber with Morgan Cross at his feet, he knew that he was one step closer to fulfilling his purpose.

He leaned down to Morgan, studying her face. She was still unconscious, but he knew that wouldn't last long. He needed to hurry. He reached into his pocket and pulled out the same knife that had taken the lives of four of the eleven. Without hesitation, he made a small incision on Morgan's left wrist, letting the blood drip onto the floor.

She let out a little yelp and moved her head slightly. She was starting to come to, her breath more regular, her head still tilting.

He muttered a quick prayer and stood up, looking at the ceiling. He couldn't help but feel a sense of excitement. The messiah was coming, and he would be the one to bring him forth.

He could not kill her yet. Her blood on the floor was just the start. He'd needed to incapacitate her for that. But she would need to be aware of her death. She would need to know why she was being offered up for this final act to work.

"Agent Cross," he muttered into the dimly lit chamber, "wake up. It's time to do your part."

She muttered something, but he wasn't sure what it was.

He was quite anxious for her to open her eyes...and not just to bring his work to a close. But he had one thing to tell her, an answer he hoped might make her more willing to play the part he'd reserved for her.

He thought that she was ready to sacrifice herself, deep down. After all, she'd willingly come back to this place. Surely, after having discovered it earlier in the day, she'd know the significance and importance of it. She knew what this place was, and she had come to him.

Yes, deep down, she was ready and willing. Soon, she'd see what she'd truly spent those ten years waiting for.

Smiling in the dark, the man who called himself Samson sat patiently beside the stirring body of Morgan Cross and waited.

CHAPTER TWENTY THREE

When she came to, there was a paralyzing moment when Morgan was certain she was still in prison. She was still in her cell, she was still locked away from the world, and the chase for Samson and the reunion with Derik over the last two days had been nothing more than a fanciful dream. Kimmy Byers would be waiting for her in the cafeteria, wanting to share one of her insane theories on world religions.

But no…somewhere off near the corners of her consciousness, she knew she was not in prison. She had a faint idea of where she was…an idea that grew more resolute with every moment she drew closer to becoming awake and aware.

Samson had been here. He'd surprised her from behind, had attacked her and…

And then what?

She knew all she had to do was open her eyes to find out. But the darkness and the sort of in-between place she inhabited was nice. The real world was on one side of the veil, and a dark and malleable place was on the other side.

She sensed that if there were memories of prison on that other side, surely there must be other memories.

As if summoned by the mere thought of such memories, Morgan caught the flicking image of her father. He was helping her into a small aluminum boat as she held a fishing rod. Morgan knew the day she was remembering, and her heart filled with a little flood of joy as she allowed herself to peek in at that memory.

She'd never been good at fishing. She'd never really had the patience. But that day out on the river had been perfect. Nothing of any real significance had happened, but it was one of the happiest days of her life. And in that dark, disconnected place, she let herself sink into it.

As she was lost in that memory, Morgan felt a warmth envelop her. But it wasn't the warmth of the sun or the feeling of a summer breeze. It was a warmth that came from something else—someone else. It was a reminder that in the real world, she wasn't alone in the cave. But she didn't want to face that. She did everything she could to bring back the memory of that little fishing trip with her father.

But that memory shifted, as memories often do. She was in a hospital room, holding her mother's hand. There were tubes and machines beeping around them and her mother's face was pale and drawn. Morgan could feel the sadness and the grief like a physical weight on her chest.

And then the memory shifted again, quick and jarring. She was in a cemetery, standing over a small gravestone. The sun was shining down on her, and the grass was green, but Morgan couldn't shake off the feeling of sadness that washed over her like a wave.

But that train of memory was soon interrupted as she felt a sharp stinging pain in her left wrist. Her eyes shot open, and she gasped, trying to sit up. She just barely saw Samson, a murky shape in the darkness.

"What...what are you doing?" she asked, her voice hoarse and weak. She started using her right hand to feel around for her Glock, hoping it was within her reach.

Samson leaned in, his face almost touching hers. "It's time, Agent Cross," he said, his voice low and intense.

She looked into his face and saw the last ten years. She saw his features, the worn down, crazy look of him. But his blue eyes were sincere somehow. He had no idea that what he was doing was insane. She was almost let down by how normal he looked.

Morgan tried to pull away from him, but her body still felt sluggish from the attack. "Time for what?" she asked, her eyes narrowing as she locked onto his gaze.

Samson didn't answer. Instead he reached out and brushed a stray strand of hair from her face. Morgan shuddered at his touch, but at the same time, she couldn't help but feel almost drawn to him...not in any romantic or respectful way. No, there was something else. Some sort of connection she felt between them. This was the man she'd been chasing for so long, the man that had felt like a failure hanging over her head during her decade in prison. There was something about the way he looked at her, as if he knew her better than anyone else ever could.

Morgan's heart raced as she looked down at her wrist, seeing the open wound and the blood staining the floor. Dimly, she had an idea of what this meant...she knew what Samson was planning to do. She guessed he had plans for her to somehow be part of the closing of his ritual.

"You have to know this is insanity," she said. "You're no messiah. You're a murderer, plain and simple."

But Samson only laughed. He made no move to come to her, apparently feeling confident that she wasn't interested in fighting him in that moment. "I've never claimed to be a messiah, Agent Cross. I'm a prophet. And I'm here to bring about the end of this world and the start of a much better one."

Morgan's heart sank as she realized the full extent of Samson's delusion. He truly believed he was doing the right thing...that he was playing a part in some sort of divine plan.

And now, he was about to sacrifice her for it.

Of course, she had no intention of allowing that to happen. Even if she couldn't find the Glock, she had no problem imagining herself beating the hell out of him. She'd felt his strength when he'd grabbed her from behind and choked her out. But this time, he wouldn't take her by surprise. And face-to-face, with no real advantage other than whatever he'd cut her with, she liked her chances.

"Before this happens, I'd like to tell you why you ended up in prison."

That simple comment disarmed her.

She moved slightly, propping herself on her right forearm. She tested her left arm while doing it, not sure how deep the cut was. There was still a stinging pain there, but she had function of the limb, at that was the important thing.

"You made it look like I was helping you," she said. "You made it—"

"Oh, no, no...not me. No, Agent Cross. I did indeed murder that fourth victim. I will gladly and proudly admit to that. But here's a little secret. The night I enacted the fourth sign, there was someone else there that night, in her house. I thought I was going to have to kill them, too. But they simply stepped out of my way and let me continue my work."

"Bullshit. I don't believe you."

"Oh, I don't care one way or the other. But if you think very hard about it...I needed you to make sure I had a driving force. You made me better at what I did. You made me want to ensure I gave this work everything. Without you on my trail, I had no real push. I'd be just another maniac out there killing people." It was dim in the chamber, but she managed to see his smile when he added: "Think about it, Agent Cross. Why do you think I stopped my work when you were away? I needed you. The last thing I would have ever wanted was for you to go to prison. While you waited, I waited. We need one another, you and I. For this work to be finished, we have to work together."

Morgan felt momentarily sick. He was right. While she didn't buy a single aspect of what Samson considered "his work," it did always strike her as odd that he'd stopped when she was in prison. It made her wonder how early into his series of murders he had decided he wanted her to be the final act.

"Who was it?"

"Oh, I don't know that. They were gone when I was done."

"And how did you make it look like I did it? Why was I framed?"

"I just told you," he said. "I don't know. It wasn't me. I never did it. I never *would* have. Did you not hear what I said just now? I *needed* you."

In the darkness, she did her best to ignore the pain in her left arm, the sticky flow of her blood. She tried to think of that fourth victim. A woman in a well-to-do neighborhood, killed in a small home library. Bludgeoned with a wine bottle and then stabbed for good measure...the wine bottle illustrating the sign of Christ turning water to wine.

She recalled the woman's name, Sandra Berryhill the set-up in the house, bringing to mind everything she could process about that particular crime scene. And then it hit her. The woman's husband had been out of town that night. He'd been on a business trip to Chicago. And he'd come back the next day to find his wife dead. Only, the details of that trip had never been confirmed by the husband's employer. Not that it mattered. Samson had left his note, so it was assumed that he'd done the killing.

Until, of course, evidence surfaced that pointed at Morgan. Evidence she'd always assumed Samson had planted there.

"The husband?" she said.

"I don't know. I suppose it would make sense." He sighed deeply and positioned himself to his knees. "I simply thought you should know that I had nothing to do with what happened to you. I was just as shocked as you were."

Shocked, she thought. *Sure.*

But deep down, she thought he was telling the truth. As much as she hated to think it, there was a bit of logic to what he'd revealed to her.

Her right hand continued to search for the Glock but all she felt was the cold, unforgiving rock floor. Of course he would have taken it and hidden it away. But he wasn't going to use it on her. No, that would be too easy. If she was to be the last sacrifice to bring about his messiah, it would need to be truly special.

"My poor, dear Agent Cross," Samson said, watching as she reached around for the Glock. "I think not. I've removed your gun. And this…well, this is where we say goodbye."

And with that, with no other form of warning, Samson raised his knife into the air with both hands, directly over his head.

This was to be the death blow…the final act to bring his work to an end. The reality of it nearly froze her but in the last moment, Morgan drew back her right foot and sent it out hard. She connected with Samson's chest and the chamber was filled with a sound like the beat of a bass drum.

He let out a wrecked coughing noise as he was thrown back into the wall behind him. Morgan sat up and watched him stumble. In doing so, she saw the Glock; Samson had stuffed it unceremoniously into the waist of his pants. She could see it poking out along his lower back.

Though it took her eyes a split second too long to get adjusted to the wavering light, she launched herself at him anyway. The tunnel was narrow so she knew she was going to hit him. She made sure to drive her knee into his ribs, knowing it stood the highest chance of causing the most damage in such a confined space. As she attacked, she saw the flame from the candle, saw shadows dancing along the walls, and the shape of Samson writhing beneath her.

She fumbled along his back as they wrestled for position, trying to gain the advantage. She got to it rather easily, though when Samson realized what she was doing, he fought harder. He allowed himself to fall back to the floor, attempting to crush her. But by then, she'd freed the Glock and, though the rock floor against her back sent a flare of pain up her spine, she did her best to remain in control as Samson pushed himself away and off of her for better position.

She leveled the Glock and pulled the trigger at the exact same time Samson attempted to flee. He dove into a small tunnel entrance to his left, letting out a scream of pain that was almost entirely drowned out by the echo of the gun going off in the tight, enclosed space.

Morgan even cried out a bit. The sound of the shot down here in the mines was deafening. For several seconds, as she scrambled to her feet, she could hear nothing. But as she started to move toward that tunnel, also thinking to stop and grab the flashlight she'd dropped at some point, her ears began to ring, and sound started to slowly come back to her.

She moved forward so quickly that she nearly collided with the wall. She steadied the gun out in front of her with her right arm as her left wrist continued to bleed. Blood trickled down from her fingers as she pivoted into the tunnel.

She'd hoped Samson would be lying there on the floor, close to death from her gunshot. But the truth of the matter was that she had no idea if she'd even hit him. For all she knew, the scream she'd heard could have been one of shock, surprise, or fear.

She held her breath and tried to listen for footfalls. But all she could hear was the resounding echo of the gunshot still filling her ears.

She had no other choice. She had to go after him. She'd nearly gotten the drop on him once today in these very same tunnels, and she'd be damned if she would let him get away again.

With her ears still filled with the echo of the shot, Morgan once again found herself exploring the unfamiliar tunnels, holding a gun and a flashlight in front of her as if to ward off the oncoming darkness.

CHAPTER TWENTY FOUR

Perhaps it was because she'd already been in these mines once today…or maybe it was because her brain still hadn't taken in the proper amount of oxygen to get back into complete working order…but Morgan couldn't help but feel as if all of these tunnels were connected in some sort of long, never-ending loop.

She had come through two tunnels so far, each opening getting slightly smaller. Oddly enough, the only thing that kept her from freaking out and losing her mind about being so far down in the earth were the little benches and tables set up in the chambers she passed by—little alcoves with candles and melted wax.

She kept her flashlight low to the floor as she chased after Samson. She knew it would be foolish to turn it off completely, but she also didn't want to hold the light directly up in front of her, straight ahead. He knew these tunnels much better than she did. And she was not going to make the same mistake she'd already made.

By keeping her flashlight low to the floor, she found that wherever he was headed, Samson appeared to be bleeding. She could only assume her shot had hit him. The question, of course, was whether it had simply been a glancing shot or if it had done some real damage. There were just enough splatters of blood on the floor to follow. She wasn't able to judge the severity of the wound based on the blood on the floor, but she took some solace in knowing that he was going to be slower and more cautious.

So she continued on, feeling fortunate that there were no branches in the tunnel. This, however, only lasted for several more seconds. She came to an intersection where two tunnels that led straight into pitch-black darkness presented themselves.

"Shit," she muttered.

If she chose wrong, Samson would get away. And then somehow, they'd have to start all over. She knew he thought she was important for this last stage. That made her think he would not give up. One way or the other, they were going to finish this tragic little play down here in the dark tunnels.

118

She trained the flashlight beam on the stone floor and saw two splotches of fresh, wet blood at the mouth of the tunnel on the left. She sneered and said, "Got you."

With a bit of new determination in her stride, Morgan entered the tunnel on the left, once again stepping into unknown darkness in search of a killer.

Her eyes were wide, and her hands were shaking. Her chest felt like it had weights tied to it, preventing her from taking a deep breath. And her stomach had tied itself into a tight, painful knot. She didn't like losing control like this, but it was difficult to stay calm as the tunnels seemed to grow thinner all around her.

"Come on, come on," she mumbled, figuring she had to be only a few feet behind him.

She held her gun out in front of her and followed the trail of blood that he'd left on the ground. Soon, she came to another intersection. And then another.

But still, no Samson.

Her mind was spinning with several possible scenarios. He could be lurking in one of these rooms, waiting for her. She could very well be walking right toward him. Or, if she had truly been that lucky, he could have stopped to bandage himself up somehow and she could be closer to him than she thought.

As she looked into more of the alcoves, she wondered how long ago it was that these mines had been used. It was certainly before they were closed. She stopped quickly in one of the little rooms and looked over the candlewax, shining her flashlight down on it. There was a sheen of dust on it. The wax was old...years old. That spoke to the fact that Samson had been down here a lot in the last several years.

Or maybe even the other man in the home of the fourth victim...maybe Sandra Berryhill's husband. But that was a mystery for another time. That was a—

She saw him up ahead. Samson. He had stopped to catch his breath, slightly hunched over in the tunnel roughly a dozen or so feet ahead of her.

"Samson!" she roared.

"Yes...I'm...I'm done, Agent Cross. Bleeding...I can't...can't..."

She advanced on him, the Glock still held out in front of her. "Get on your knees," she ordered.

"I can't. Hurts...too much. The shot...right in the guts. I...please help."

It was peculiar, but she felt in that moment that it was more important for Samson to come out of this alive. If there was indeed one other person involved in her framing, maybe Samson knew more than he'd revealed. She stepped forward cautiously, realizing that she had no real options here. She had more or less trapped herself. If she cuffed him, there was no way in hell she could march him out if he was injured this badly.

Besides, killing him would be too easy. She hadn't waited ten years to simply off him in a darkened cave. No, she wanted answers. She deserved answers.

More than that, what would her father think? If there was a way to end this without killing Samson, she had to take it. She had to try.

She took one more step toward him, the barrel of the gun no more than two feet from him. In the flashlight beam, she could see the pain in his eyes.

And a smile on his lips.

In an instant, he stood up straight and tossed something into her face. Sand or a powder of some kind. And as she stumbled back, screaming out and instinctually bringing her hands to her face, she recalled that he had the knife. He had played her like a damn fiddle, and he still had the knife.

Her eyes stung. They were burning terribly. She'd only been blinded for a few moments, but when she opened her eyes again the world was so dark, she couldn't see a thing. She tried to use what sight she still had left to get a bead on him, but all she could see were faint blobs of light.

The son of a bitch had blinded her with sand or some other particulate matter. Yes, she still had the Glock, but the quarters were too tight, too contained.

"Come on!" she screamed. Ten years of frustration came out in the scream and in that moment, she didn't care if she died. She didn't care if he plunged that knife into her throat, chest, stomach. She didn't care. She just wanted this to be over.

As she did her best to blink the sand or powder away, her eyes had to once again get adjusted to the natural darkness of the tunnel. A flickering blob of gray came rushing forward as Samson shoved her hard against the wall. The wind went rushing out of her, the back of her head banged off of the rock, and her hand released the gun.

She heard it clatter to the floor and with it, she also felt her last hope relinquished.

120

"Come on already," she said, barely able to push the words out of her lungs.

The lack of caring suddenly evaporated, replaced with anger. And when she sensed him coming close again, still little more than a gray blur in her vision, she let out a right-handed jab. She felt his nose beneath her knuckles, cracking and bleeding instantly. But at the same time, she felt the blade of the knife come down. It sliced across her right wrist, digging deep, clanging against bone.

She howled.

Morgan hit the ground, screaming out in pain. She could feel the warm liquid seeping out of her wrist, both arms now losing blood. The gun...she had to find the gun. She twisted and turned and started to crawl in search of the gun, but the pain was unbearable.

The rough ground ripped through her hands and the blood made it hard to keep traction. She sensed him moving somewhere behind her, maybe even with the blade pointed over his head for the death blow.

But before that could happen, she heard something else in the tunnel. Thunder? A small quake?

No...it was footsteps. Rapidly approaching footsteps. And in their wake, the bouncing glare of a flashlight beam.

"Drop the knife and get on your knees!"

Derik. It was Derik. Somehow, he'd found his way back to her. Maybe he'd come to the same conclusion she had...that Samson's endgame was to take place in these mines.

She felt something bump into her and she didn't even try to stop herself from falling down. When her chest hit the floor, all she was truly aware of was how difficult it was to breathe and the feeling of blood leaving her body—not just from both her forearms, but now also from a spot on her left cheek as her face struck the rock floor.

She heard the skirmish just behind her. She heard Samson cry out, heard Derik hiss and then curse. The last thing she heard was what sounded like a meaty thud, like a steak being slapped down on a butcher's block.

After that, things went quiet. She was pretty sure she heard Derik say her name a single time, shaky and weak.

"Morgan?"

She opened her mouth to answer, to tell him that she was okay. But before a single word escaped her lips, she felt herself falling back into that place where memories of her parents waited for her...for better or for worse.

CHAPTER TWENTY FIVE

Voices and sluggish movement. That was everything that made up Morgan's world for a brief moment in time.

Morgan knew she was walking. She was aware of her muscles working, of her knees bending and carrying her back through the tunnels. But there were also arms and hands helping her along. Several different sets, from what she could tell.

"Derik?" she asked as she opened her still-stinging eyes to the tunnels. Everything was still dark, still a work of rough rock and the occasional alcove with partially used candles.

"Yeah, I'm here," he said from behind her.

"Are you okay?"

"Yeah. I'm fine. You?"

She wasn't sure how to answer. Hell, she felt almost too tired to think about it. So in the end, the answer she gave was: "I'm bleeding. And I can't see."

"Do you need to stop?"

She actually chuckled at this. "No," she said. "Get me the hell out of here."

The combination of knowing that she was headed out of the mines and that Derik was there made it a bit easier to breathe. Her senses started to come back to her and before too long, she was pretty sure she could smell and even taste fresh air somewhere up ahead. As her thoughts became less muddied, hundreds of questions presented themselves.

"Derik?" she asked, still not quite sure where he was in proximity to her.

"Yes?"

"Where's Samson?"

"He's cuffed and about ten feet ahead of us. There are three other officers here. Can you...can you really not see?"

"No. Just murky shapes. He threw something in my eyes."

"And cut you up pretty bad, too. But we bandaged them up as well as we could."

"Yeah, how did you find—"

"Save your breath," he said. "Wait until we're out of here, okay?"

That sounded like a great idea. She continued trying to test her vision and though it seemed to be getting a bit better, the darkness and jostling of several different flashlights made it hard to focus. It was hard to tell, but it felt like she was being supported by two sets of arms on either side of her. As the blurry gray shapes became a bit more defined, she turned her head, looking for Derik. She found him, staring at her with worried eyes as they made their way out of the mines. She could hear the rest of the officers talking up ahead.

But she didn't hear Samson, and she wasn't sure how to feel about that.

The feel and smell of fresh air increased and after several more moments, they came to a stop. She peered ahead and saw that they had come to the entrance to the mines. Though, in the time since she'd entered earlier, someone had torn much of the barricade down. A gorgeous, clear night waited on the other side of the now mostly opened blockage.

"When we get out, I want to sit down," she said.

"Absolutely," Derik answered. When she looked over to him, she saw a new bandage on his head, and she wondered how he was feeling. Maybe coming back down into the mines after what had happened to him earlier in the day wasn't the best idea. But she respected the hell out of him for doing it.

She found that the barricade had been destroyed enough for her to pretty much walk straight out. When she stepped out into the night, the first thing she saw was a small group of police officers a few feet away from the mine entrance. Two of them held flashlights and one of them came rushing over to the officers ahead of Morgan and Derik.

She saw Samson between them, his hands cuffed behind his back. He was walking with a hunch, but remained quiet. Morgan started after him, somehow feeling that whatever was going on between them wasn't over. She still needed answers, and he still needed to understand that whatever he'd had planned for her had ultimately failed.

"Nope," Derik said. "You sit."

She didn't need much more urging. She took one more step and then took a seat in the tall grass along the outer rim of the mine. She looked down at her arms and saw that they'd been bandaged in a makeshift way. Was that a shirt on her right arm, torn into ribbons and wrapped around it? She thought so. And when she finally took a good look at Derik and saw that he only had a T-shirt on, that was all the answer she needed.

"Thank you," she said.

"Yeah. I mean, did I have a choice?" Derik asked, sitting beside her.

"Does Mueller know you're here?"

"He does now. I called him when I realized where you were."

"How did you know where I was, anyway?"

"The truth? There's a small tracer tucked behind your badge in your badge holder. There was also one on your phone but...well, you sort of destroyed that."

"Mueller's been tracking me the entire time?"

"It was Mueller's idea. But I've been the one in charge of making sure I know where you go."

She knew she should be slightly upset about this, but it didn't seem important in that moment. There were so many other things that took priority over Mueller feeling the need to keep tabs on her. And really...she couldn't blame him.

"Samson...I think I shot him...is he going to live?"

"You got him high in the shoulder. I think you shattered his collarbone. He says that entire area is numb. Other than that...he's okay. But really...is that what you're worried about? That the maniac is still alive?"

"Maybe," Morgan said. A bird chirped nearby, and she found herself turning her head to look at it. "What happens now?"

"We take him in."

"And then what? I'm really afraid there's....there's more to the story. I think there might have been another man involved."

"What? Why?"

"Because Samson told me. And he had a point. It goes back to the fourth victim...when I was framed. It's..."

"We can talk about that later."

"I had the chance to kill him," Morgan said, the words coming unexpectedly. "I could have done it. And now I wonder...did I make the right call?"

"Professionally, yes. I'd say so."

She was silent for a moment, trying to put her feelings into words. But it all came crashing down on her at once. She rested her head against Derik's shoulder and started to cry.

"Hey, hey," he said, putting his arm around her. "It's okay! Everything is going to be fine. Just take a breath."

"No, it's not. Will it?"

"What do you mean?"

"The anger I felt down there…it was scary. When it was just the two of us in the dark…I think I felt his humanity. I know that sounds weird, but…Derik, I really don't think he had a hand in framing me."

He nodded and she could tell he wanted to explore what she meant by that, but he remained quiet. As they sat in silence together, another cop came over and handed Morgan a bottle of water.

When the other cop was gone, Morgan twisted the top off of the water and took three deep gulps, nearly choking on it.

"If you believe that, then I say we need to look into it," Derik said. "But not right now. Right now, I think we need to get you to a hospital. Both of those cuts on your arms might need stitches. I know for certain the right one will."

"Yeah, okay. Just…give me a second, will you? I'd really just like to sit and zone out for a second, you know?"

"Do you feel okay?"

She wasn't quite sure how to answer that. She looked up at the night sky, speckled with stars and all held together by a moon that was three-quarters full. Staring up at it, she nearly started to cry again. It made no sense at first, but she then understood that it had been ten years since she sat under a sky this big, this wide. It had been ten years since she'd experienced any sort of freedom on this scale.

"I'm not sure," she finally answered. "But I think I'm going to be."

"So…awkward question," Derik said. "You're clearly going through something right now. Like, in this very moment. Do you want me to leave you alone? Maybe see what I can do to help up at the cars?"

She shook her head. She had no romantic interest in Derik, and other than that one kiss had never seen him in that light. But in the moment, he was all she had. Sure, Skunk was waiting for her back at the house, but that was different. For right now, he was still Lora's. And maybe he would always be Lora's.

She found herself getting emotional over the situation, so she shut it down. Not now…not here.

"I'd actually like it if you'd stay for a while. And…and maybe forgot what I said about another man being there with the fourth victim. I don't know what I want to do with that yet."

Startled, Derik asked: "Are you sure?"

"No, not really. But all the same…" She ended the comment with a shrug.

They sat side by side under the night sky as Morgan began to get control of herself. The tears stopped, but the stinging pain in her wrists continued. She peered up at the stars, breathing in the night and relishing the feel of all that space around her.

Morgan felt herself begin to relax for the first time in what felt like forever. She was still grappling with everything that had happened, but for now she was content to just sit in the grass with Derik and stare up at the stars.

"I'm sorry," Derik said suddenly.

"For what?"

"For everything. For getting you into this mess. Mueller presented the idea to me just like he presented it to the others, and I could have said no."

"But he and Yen would have overruled you."

"Maybe. But still…I don't feel like it was right for me to agree to it. No offense, but I don't think you were quite ready."

She smiled at him and said, "Our killer is in custody. Seems like I was perfectly ready. Now," she said, playfully slapping at his knee, "get me to the hospital so I can get stitched up."

He got to his feet and helped her up. Together, they walked through the tall grass, back up to where she had parked about two hours ago. There were four police cars sitting there, and lights tearing the night apart. And in the midst of them, already placed into the back seat of a patrol car, she spotted Samson.

He spotted her as well and they locked eyes. And even after she tore her gaze away from him, she was overcome with the sickening feeling that this probably wouldn't be the last time she saw him.

CHAPTER TWENTY SIX

The cuts on both of her wrists were healing well, but there was still a strange itching sensation whenever she stretched her arms to their full extent. In the last few days, it had been especially noticeable whenever she extended her arm to paint.

It had been fifteen days since she and Derik, along with some other officers, had come out of the mines with Samson, the Seven Signs Killer. There were a variety of reasons Morgan had laid low since then, and her injuries were only a small part of it.

So, while she waited for things to cool down, she decided to fix up her father's house. It was tiring work, but she found that she actually enjoyed it.

As she scraped off old wallpaper and painted over the dingy yellow walls, Morgan's mind kept drifting back to the case. She couldn't shake off the feeling that there was something more to it, something they had missed. She was sure that Samson was the killer, but what if there was someone else involved? What if she had missed something crucial?

It was possible. After all, nearly everyone had overlooked the convenient fact that the husband of the fourth victim had been away for work...and that his manager had never been able to fully back it up. Somehow, in the fever of a manhunt for the serial killer, that had gone overlooked.

She doubted much about the case to come would get overlooked, though. Derik had texted her yesterday to tell her that the news was painting her as a superhero. She was a controversial figure (some still thought she'd somehow had a hand in the killings, though the police were working hard to get the word out that the murders for the killer's fifth sign occurred three days before she'd been released from prison. It was also common knowledge that she'd been the one to track Samson down in the mines and had played the biggest part in his capture).

On top of that pressure, she also had Mueller breathing down her neck. In a very odd twist, he'd reamed her for going off alone into such a dangerous situation. He's also eventually read Derik the riot act for following after her, given that he'd been diagnosed with a concussion that same day. Yet, Mueller seemed to understand her commitment to her job; he'd offered her a new contract, essentially officially returning her status as a special agent. His only caveat was that she couldn't start for another three months. He wanted her to get acclimated to normal life first.

And that was fine with her. She could fix her father's house up. She could try to get used to advancements in technology that she was still slightly baffled by…things like streaming services that were essentially just a fancy return to cable, doorbell cameras, AI-driven art and writing software, and an overabundance of movie remakes, reboots, and sequels.

It was one of those things that made ten years seem like an insurmountable amount of time while also being nothing more than a little blip on the radar of life.

On that fifteenth day after coming out of the mines, she was in the middle of working in the kitchen when she heard a car door close from outside. She had the door propped open to allow the paint fumes out, so she heard it clearly.

She wiped the sweat off her brow and walked to the front door. She was surprised to see Derik walking up the sidewalk. She was even more surprised to see that he was carrying a small cooler and a pail filled with paint rollers.

"Hey," he said, a sheepish grin on his face. "I've come to help."

"But I didn't ask for help."

"Which makes my gesture so much more heroic and dashing. What are we painting today?"

She smiled and opened the door all the way, allowing him in. "The kitchen."

"I brought sodas," he said, lifting up the little cooler.

"Got anything harder?"

Derik laughed and shook his head. "Not at this hour, but I have the best ginger ale you can get on the market."

Morgan couldn't help but smirk. "In that case, you're hired."

He walked in and looked around, taking in the state of the house. "Wow, you've really done a lot of work here."

"Yeah, I have. It's been…therapeutic," she said, realizing how cliché it sounded.

"No, I get it," he said, nodding. "So, how have you been?"

She shrugged. "Okay, I guess. Trying to keep busy. How about you?"

"Good. Mostly worried about you. And much like the last time I came to this house, I came bearing news."

"Not another case, I assume," she said with a laugh.

Derik smirked. "Well…"

Skunk had made his way into the room to sniff at the visitor. He wagged his tail as Derik scratched his head with one hand and opened up the cooler with the other. He plucked a ginger ale out and handed it to Morgan. She popped the top instantly and took a huge drink.

She hadn't had a ginger ale in ten years. Although she wished it were something harder, the sweetness was a welcome addition to her palate.

"Well what?" she asked, afraid that he truly was being serious.

"I've been sent to invite you to a meeting. Mueller doesn't know about it yet. It's coming from a bit higher up."

"From who?"

"Deputy Director Irvin. He wants to meet with you, and I don't think he wants Mueller to know."

"Why?"

"I have no idea. That's literally all I know. Well, that, and the fact that I'm apparently just an errand boy. Sort of a liaison between you and the bureau. He's going to send you an email sometime this week and I've been asked to make sure you respond to it. Apparently, you haven't been answering ones from Mueller or Yen."

"That would be correct."

As they began to paint the walls, Morgan's mind raced with the possibilities. And that, on its own, was monumental. Because it had been a very long time since she'd had any sort of possibilities at all.

It had her daring to think that the future might just break her way after all.

***

The meeting was a week later. The house was painted, and she'd even put in new kitchen cabinets. Her shoulders were sore, and her back was screaming bloody murder at her, but the manual labor had done her some good.

The meeting was not in the usual building where she'd always reported for work. This office was two blocks over, in a satellite office away from the field office. Morgan had only ever been there for conferences and team drills. When she arrived there, she took the elevator to the third floor as her email had directed.

As the elevator doors opened, Morgan found herself in a sleek, modern office space. The walls were glass, and the furniture was all minimalist and high-end. It was a far cry from the drab, government-issued furnishings of the FBI's main building.

A young woman in a sharp black pantsuit greeted her at the door with a smile. "Agent Cross, welcome. Please follow me."

Morgan followed the woman into a conference room where she was greeted by Deputy Director Irvin, a man she had only seen a handful of times in her career. He was a tall, imposing figure with a sharp jawline and piercing blue eyes. He didn't look particularly pleased to see her.

"Agent Cross. Thank you for coming." His voice was cold and formal. He gestured to the small conference table in the middle of the room and said, "Please have a seat."

Morgan sat down, feeling a bit nervous. She had no idea what this meeting was about, and the fact that Deputy Director Irvin himself had requested it made her even more uneasy. It didn't help that they were the only two in the room.

Morgan nodded, taking a seat at the conference table. "Of course. Though I have no idea why I'm here."

Irvin sat down across from her and leaned across the table slightly. "I'll get straight to the point. Before your time in prison, did you enjoy your time with the BAU?"

"I did. Yes, sir."

"And other than his not coming to your side immediately when the shit hit the fan, did you ever have any grievances with AD Mueller?"

She considered the answer for a moment and decided to be as honest as possible. "He was never an easy man to work for. He would be friendly and helpful one day and then almost spiteful the next. I will say, though, that it wasn't until my trial came around that I ever actually felt as if he never had my best interest in mind."

"I could see that, absolutely. Now, as for you…first and foremost, I understand that you've been through a lot recently," Irvin said, leaning back in his chair. "You've been through a traumatic experience, and I want to make sure that you're okay."

Morgan nodded, not sure where this was going. "I'm okay, thank you for your concern."

"Good. But I'm not just here to check on your well-being. I'm here to offer you a job."

Morgan frowned. "Mueller already offered me a spot back."

"Yes, but he wanted you on a lengthy probation period first," Irvin said. "Mueller doesn't know, but I'm going over his head. I want you back in, Morgan, sooner than later."

Confusion flitted through Morgan's mind. She'd thought she was still in hot water, not exactly desired here, at least according to Mueller. "Sir, I appreciate that, but can I ask why?"

He drew a breath. "Well, I don't know if you've been paying attention to the news, but people are becoming very sympathetic to you. The details of your case are coming back up and a whistleblower somewhere within the bureau has released details about how sloppily and lazily things were handled when it came to proclaiming your innocence. And a lot of that falls on Mueller."

"Oh," she said, surprised that she almost felt guilty about this.

"He'll be notified of this tomorrow, so I'd appreciate your discretion until then. Mueller has good standing with the FBI, but this one's my call." Irvin leaned forward, his expression softening slightly. "Listen, Cross, I'll be straight with you. I think you deserve a second chance. I believe that you have what it takes to lead, someday. You've already proven that you're a talented agent. And I think you have the drive and determination to make a real difference here. I want you working as a Special Agent here in the Dallas office."

Morgan considered his words carefully. It was true that she had always aspired to a leadership position within the bureau, back when she had dreams of the future, before she'd been locked away. And the prospect of working alongside Derik again in an official capacity was certainly appealing. But she also knew that this offer came with a lot of risk.

"What about the other agents in the Dallas office? Won't they feel like I'm being given special treatment?"

Irvin nodded. "There will be some resentment, I'm sure. But the truth is, there's already some tension among the agents here. And I think that having a strong, capable agent like you around could actually help ease some of that tension. Whether you want to accept it or not, you're a celebrity at the moment. I think everyone here knows it would make sense to give you such a role. And with Agent Greene…I feel very good about this decision. You two make a great team. Would be a shame to let it all go to waste."

She nodded and then had a powerful thought—a thought that basically made the decision for her.

Working in the department again meant access to great resources and research. And even with Mueller sniffing around, she clearly had the favor of her higher-ups. She could use this.

It meant she would be able to look into who framed her without fear of being caught or stopped by higher-ups.

"When would I start?" she asked.

"I do agree with Mueller on this. You need some time to adjust…though I think three months might be a bit much. If you were to accept this job, I'd ask you to begin when you're ready. Weeks, months. The decision is yours."

She pretended to think it over, though her mind was already made up.

She'd be starting right away.

Morgan smiled across the table and offered her hand. "Thank you, sir. I can't wait to get started."

NOW AVAILABLE!

FOR RAGE
(A Morgan Cross FBI Suspense Thriller—Book Two)

Bodies turning up in hedge mazes. A killer taunting the FBI. An ex-con FBI agent determined to stop a killer—while also closing in on who framed her….

"A masterpiece of thriller and mystery."
—Books and Movie Reviews, Roberto Mattos (re Once Gone)

FOR RAGE is book #2 in a long-anticipated new series by #1 bestseller and USA Today bestselling author Blake Pierce, whose bestseller Once Gone (a free download) has received over 7,000 five star ratings and reviews.

Superstar FBI Agent Morgan Cross was at the height of her career when she was framed, wrongly imprisoned, and sent to do 10 hard years in prison. Finally exonerated and set free, Morgan emerges from jail as a changed person—hardened, ruthless, closed off to the world, and unsure how to start again. When the FBI comes knocking, desperately needing Morgan to return and hunt down a killer leaving bodies in hedge mazes, Morgan is torn.

Morgan is not the same person, no longer willing to play by the rules, and will stop at nothing this time. In a non-stop thriller, it will be a deadly cat and mouse chase between a diabolical killer and an ex-con FBI agent who has nothing left to lose—with a new victim's fate riding on it all.

A page-turning and harrowing crime thriller featuring a brilliant and tortured FBI agent, the Morgan Cross series is a riveting mystery, packed with non-stop action, suspense, twists and turns, revelations, and driven by a breakneck pace that will keep you flipping pages late into the night. Fans of Rachel Caine, Teresa Driscoll and Robert Dugoni are sure to fall in love.

Future books in the series are also available!

"An edge of your seat thriller in a new series that keeps you turning pages! ...So many twists, turns and red herrings... I can't wait to see what happens next."
—Reader review (Her Last Wish)

"A strong, complex story about two FBI agents trying to stop a serial killer. If you want an author to capture your attention and have you guessing, yet trying to put the pieces together, Pierce is your author!"
—Reader review (Her Last Wish)

"A typical Blake Pierce twisting, turning, roller coaster ride suspense thriller. Will have you turning the pages to the last sentence of the last chapter!!!"
—Reader review (City of Prey)

"Right from the start we have an unusual protagonist that I haven't seen done in this genre before. The action is nonstop... A very atmospheric novel that will keep you turning pages well into the wee hours."
—Reader review (City of Prey)

"Everything that I look for in a book... a great plot, interesting characters, and grabs your interest right away. The book moves along at a breakneck pace and stays that way until the end. Now on go I to book two!"
—Reader review (Girl, Alone)

"Exciting, heart pounding, edge of your seat book... a must read for mystery and suspense readers!"
—Reader review (Girl, Alone)

Blake Pierce

Blake Pierce is the USA Today bestselling author of the RILEY PAGE mystery series, which includes seventeen books. Blake Pierce is also the author of the MACKENZIE WHITE mystery series, comprising fourteen books; of the AVERY BLACK mystery series, comprising six books; of the KERI LOCKE mystery series, comprising five books; of the MAKING OF RILEY PAIGE mystery series, comprising six books; of the KATE WISE mystery series, comprising seven books; of the CHLOE FINE psychological suspense mystery, comprising six books; of the JESSIE HUNT psychological suspense thriller series, comprising twenty-eight books; of the AU PAIR psychological suspense thriller series, comprising three books; of the ZOE PRIME mystery series, comprising six books; of the ADELE SHARP mystery series, comprising sixteen books, of the EUROPEAN VOYAGE cozy mystery series, comprising six books; of the LAURA FROST FBI suspense thriller, comprising eleven books; of the ELLA DARK FBI suspense thriller, comprising fourteen books (and counting); of the A YEAR IN EUROPE cozy mystery series, comprising nine books, of the AVA GOLD mystery series, comprising six books; of the RACHEL GIFT mystery series, comprising ten books (and counting); of the VALERIE LAW mystery series, comprising nine books (and counting); of the PAIGE KING mystery series, comprising eight books (and counting); of the MAY MOORE mystery series, comprising eleven books; of the CORA SHIELDS mystery series, comprising eight books (and counting); of the NICKY LYONS mystery series, comprising eight books (and counting), of the CAMI LARK mystery series, comprising eight books (and counting), of the AMBER YOUNG mystery series, comprising five books (and counting), of the DAISY FORTUNE mystery series, comprising five books (and counting), of the FIONA RED mystery series, comprising five books (and counting), of the FAITH BOLD mystery series, comprising five books (and counting), of the JULIETTE HART mystery series, comprising five books (and counting), of the MORGAN CROSS mystery series, comprising five books (and counting), and of the new FINN WRIGHT mystery series, comprising five books (and counting).

An avid reader and lifelong fan of the mystery and thriller genres, Blake loves to hear from you, so please feel free to visit www.blakepierceauthor.com to learn more and stay in touch.

BOOKS BY BLAKE PIERCE

FINN WRIGHT MYSTERY SERIES
WHEN YOU'RE MINE (Book #1)
WHEN YOU'RE SAFE (Book #2)
WHEN YOU'RE CLOSE (Book #3)
WHEN YOU'RE SLEEPING (Book #4)
WHEN YOU'RE SANE (Book #5)

MORGAN CROSS MYSTERY SERIES
FOR YOU (Book #1)
FOR RAGE (Book #2)
FOR LUST (Book #3)
FOR WRATH (Book #4)
FOREVER (Book #5)

JULIETTE HART MYSTERY SERIES
NOTHING TO FEAR (Book #1)
NOTHING THERE (Book #2)
NOTHING WATCHING (Book #3)
NOTHING HIDING (Book #4)
NOTHING LEFT (Book #5)

FAITH BOLD MYSTERY SERIES
SO LONG (Book #1)
SO COLD (Book #2)
SO SCARED (Book #3)
SO NORMAL (Book #4)
SO FAR GONE (Book #5)

FIONA RED MYSTERY SERIES
LET HER GO (Book #1)
LET HER BE (Book #2)
LET HER HOPE (Book #3)
LET HER WISH (Book #4)
LET HER LIVE (Book #5)

DAISY FORTUNE MYSTERY SERIES
NEED YOU (Book #1)
CLAIM YOU (Book #2)
CRAVE YOU (Book #3)
CHOOSE YOU (Book #4)
CHASE YOU (Book #5)

AMBER YOUNG MYSTERY SERIES
ABSENT PITY (Book #1)
ABSENT REMORSE (Book #2)
ABSENT FEELING (Book #3)
ABSENT MERCY (Book #4)
ABSENT REASON (Book #5)

CAMI LARK MYSTERY SERIES
JUST ME (Book #1)
JUST OUTSIDE (Book #2)
JUST RIGHT (Book #3)
JUST FORGET (Book #4)
JUST ONCE (Book #5)
JUST HIDE (Book #6)
JUST NOW (Book #7)
JUST HOPE (Book #8)

NICKY LYONS MYSTERY SERIES
ALL MINE (Book #1)
ALL HIS (Book #2)
ALL HE SEES (Book #3)
ALL ALONE (Book #4)
ALL FOR ONE (Book #5)
ALL HE TAKES (Book #6)
ALL FOR ME (Book #7)
ALL IN (Book #8)

CORA SHIELDS MYSTERY SERIES
UNDONE (Book #1)
UNWANTED (Book #2)
UNHINGED (Book #3)
UNSAID (Book #4)

UNGLUED (Book #5)
UNSTABLE (Book #6)
UNKNOWN (Book #7)
UNAWARE (Book #8)

MAY MOORE SUSPENSE THRILLER
NEVER RUN (Book #1)
NEVER TELL (Book #2)
NEVER LIVE (Book #3)
NEVER HIDE (Book #4)
NEVER FORGIVE (Book #5)
NEVER AGAIN (Book #6)
NEVER LOOK BACK (Book #7)
NEVER FORGET (Book #8)
NEVER LET GO (Book #9)
NEVER PRETEND (Book #10)
NEVER HESITATE (Book #11)

PAIGE KING MYSTERY SERIES
THE GIRL HE PINED (Book #1)
THE GIRL HE CHOSE (Book #2)
THE GIRL HE TOOK (Book #3)
THE GIRL HE WISHED (Book #4)
THE GIRL HE CROWNED (Book #5)
THE GIRL HE WATCHED (Book #6)
THE GIRL HE WANTED (Book #7)
THE GIRL HE CLAIMED (Book #8)

VALERIE LAW MYSTERY SERIES
NO MERCY (Book #1)
NO PITY (Book #2)
NO FEAR (Book #3)
NO SLEEP (Book #4)
NO QUARTER (Book #5)
NO CHANCE (Book #6)
NO REFUGE (Book #7)
NO GRACE (Book #8)
NO ESCAPE (Book #9)

RACHEL GIFT MYSTERY SERIES

HER LAST WISH (Book #1)
HER LAST CHANCE (Book #2)
HER LAST HOPE (Book #3)
HER LAST FEAR (Book #4)
HER LAST CHOICE (Book #5)
HER LAST BREATH (Book #6)
HER LAST MISTAKE (Book #7)
HER LAST DESIRE (Book #8)
HER LAST REGRET (Book #9)
HER LAST HOUR (Book #10)

AVA GOLD MYSTERY SERIES
CITY OF PREY (Book #1)
CITY OF FEAR (Book #2)
CITY OF BONES (Book #3)
CITY OF GHOSTS (Book #4)
CITY OF DEATH (Book #5)
CITY OF VICE (Book #6)

A YEAR IN EUROPE
A MURDER IN PARIS (Book #1)
DEATH IN FLORENCE (Book #2)
VENGEANCE IN VIENNA (Book #3)
A FATALITY IN SPAIN (Book #4)

ELLA DARK FBI SUSPENSE THRILLER
GIRL, ALONE (Book #1)
GIRL, TAKEN (Book #2)
GIRL, HUNTED (Book #3)
GIRL, SILENCED (Book #4)
GIRL, VANISHED (Book 5)
GIRL ERASED (Book #6)
GIRL, FORSAKEN (Book #7)
GIRL, TRAPPED (Book #8)
GIRL, EXPENDABLE (Book #9)
GIRL, ESCAPED (Book #10)
GIRL, HIS (Book #11)
GIRL, LURED (Book #12)
GIRL, MISSING (Book #13)
GIRL, UNKNOWN (Book #14)

THE PERFECT PEOPLE (Book #27)
THE PERFECT WITNESS (Book #28)

CHLOE FINE PSYCHOLOGICAL SUSPENSE SERIES
NEXT DOOR (Book #1)
A NEIGHBOR'S LIE (Book #2)
CUL DE SAC (Book #3)
SILENT NEIGHBOR (Book #4)
HOMECOMING (Book #5)
TINTED WINDOWS (Book #6)

KATE WISE MYSTERY SERIES
IF SHE KNEW (Book #1)
IF SHE SAW (Book #2)
IF SHE RAN (Book #3)
IF SHE HID (Book #4)
IF SHE FLED (Book #5)
IF SHE FEARED (Book #6)
IF SHE HEARD (Book #7)

THE MAKING OF RILEY PAIGE SERIES
WATCHING (Book #1)
WAITING (Book #2)
LURING (Book #3)
TAKING (Book #4)
STALKING (Book #5)
KILLING (Book #6)

RILEY PAIGE MYSTERY SERIES
ONCE GONE (Book #1)
ONCE TAKEN (Book #2)
ONCE CRAVED (Book #3)
ONCE LURED (Book #4)
ONCE HUNTED (Book #5)
ONCE PINED (Book #6)
ONCE FORSAKEN (Book #7)
ONCE COLD (Book #8)
ONCE STALKED (Book #9)
ONCE LOST (Book #10)
ONCE BURIED (Book #11)

ONCE BOUND (Book #12)
ONCE TRAPPED (Book #13)
ONCE DORMANT (Book #14)
ONCE SHUNNED (Book #15)
ONCE MISSED (Book #16)
ONCE CHOSEN (Book #17)

MACKENZIE WHITE MYSTERY SERIES
BEFORE HE KILLS (Book #1)
BEFORE HE SEES (Book #2)
BEFORE HE COVETS (Book #3)
BEFORE HE TAKES (Book #4)
BEFORE HE NEEDS (Book #5)
BEFORE HE FEELS (Book #6)
BEFORE HE SINS (Book #7)
BEFORE HE HUNTS (Book #8)
BEFORE HE PREYS (Book #9)
BEFORE HE LONGS (Book #10)
BEFORE HE LAPSES (Book #11)
BEFORE HE ENVIES (Book #12)
BEFORE HE STALKS (Book #13)
BEFORE HE HARMS (Book #14)

AVERY BLACK MYSTERY SERIES
CAUSE TO KILL (Book #1)
CAUSE TO RUN (Book #2)
CAUSE TO HIDE (Book #3)
CAUSE TO FEAR (Book #4)
CAUSE TO SAVE (Book #5)
CAUSE TO DREAD (Book #6)

KERI LOCKE MYSTERY SERIES
A TRACE OF DEATH (Book #1)
A TRACE OF MURDER (Book #2)
A TRACE OF VICE (Book #3)
A TRACE OF CRIME (Book #4)
A TRACE OF HOPE (Book #5)

83200787R00085